D0922709

·THE·
C·H·I·L·L·I·N·G
HOUR

·THE·
C·H·I·L·L·I·N·G
Tales of the Real and Unreal
HOUR

COLLIN McDONALD

COBBLEHILL BOOKS

Dutton · New York

To those individuals so special to me,
present and past: you know who you are;
to kids everywhere,
and to
Florence Feiler, agent and friend.

Library of Congress Cataloging-in-Publication Data

McDonald, Collin, date
     The chilling hour : tales of the real and unreal / Collin
McDonald.
         p.   cm.
     Summary: A collection of horror stories in which some strange occurrences
happen in such otherwise ordinary settings as a ski vacation and a school field
trip.
     ISBN 0-525-65101-2
     1. Horror tales, American.   2. Children's stories, American.
[1. Horror—Fiction.   2. Supernatural—Fiction.   3. Short Stories.]
I. Title.
PZ7.M4784176Ch   1992   92-5522   CIP   AC
[Fic]—dc20

Published in the United States by Cobblehill Books,
an affiliate of Dutton Children's Books,
a division of Penguin Books USA Inc.
375 Hudson Street, New York, New York 10014

Designed by Barbara Powderly
Printed in the United States of America
First Edition   10 9 8 7 6 5 4 3 2 1

Contents

The Driver

The razor wind slipped through Jim's goose-down jacket, wool shirt, and skier's underwear as though he were wearing no clothing at all. What had seemed little more than a frisky breeze across the high Colorado Rockies just minutes before was building rapidly into a full-blown blizzard. The angry gale mixed new and old snow in endless sheets of blinding white, making it nearly impossible to see even nearby trees, let alone the mountaintop. The meandering trail above the cabin, where Jim had hoped to try his new cross-country skis, was a shapeless mass of frozen peaks and swirls.

"Some vacation," he muttered, stabbing at the release catch on the ski bindings with one of his poles. He picked up the skis, poles, and a pair of snowshoes leaning near the door and carried everything inside. His dad already had a friendly pine fire snapping in the stone fireplace.

"Whooowee!" Jim shook a powdery cloud of snow crystals from his jacket. "It's super *cold* out there!"

"Just don't make a mess with those clothes," his mother called from the kitchen alcove. "Hang your jacket by the door. I don't want wet things all over." She sniffed, and then sneezed. "Rotten cold," she added, to no one in particular.

Jim's sister, Susan, two years younger than he, was sprawled in an overstuffed chair. One of her feet, encased in a large, furry slipper with fake rabbit ears on each side, hung over an arm of the chair. "Grab me a soda from the kitchen, will you, Jimmy? I'm comfy and I don't feel like moving."

"Get it yourself," Jim growled, still knocking snow from his jacket and jeans. "Your legs work just like mine do."

She scowled at him. "Gee, what a grouch! Ma! How long do I have to stay in the same cabin with this grouch?"

"Maybe a day or two longer than we thought," their father said. "It's not so terrible, though. We have wood for the fireplace, food for a couple of days in the kitchen, and gas for the little generator in the back, so we have electricity. And fortunately your mother even thought to bring along a few games to play. So we miss a few days skiing. So what?"

"So I don't know if I want to play board games with this grizzly bear grouch," said Susan, rising slowly and heading for the kitchen.

Jim rubbed his hands together. "This really ticks me off," he grumbled. "We not only can't get over to the lifts for downhill runs, we can't even do any cross-country skiing the way the wind and the drifts are. And we can't get to the lodge to take a swim in the indoor pool, either."

"Looks like it'll get worse before it gets better," Jim's dad said, poking at the fire.

"Pretty soon we won't be able to even *find* the car outside," Jim said, staring at the flame. "Just another high mound of snow by the tree. And the Wilsons' cabin is hardly more than a speck. All I could see was part of their roof and the chimney."

"I'm sure they're fine. The plows will get up here to clear the road down to the lodge, but it just takes a while." Jim's dad rose and turned toward the kitchen. "So . . . anybody for a game?"

Later, as they roasted marshmallows over the still-crackling fire, Susan said, "You know, I'm kind of scared."

"No need to be," their dad said. "We have food and we can stay warm. No big deal. In a day or so, the plows will open the road from the valley and we can head over to the lodge and the lifts or we can head back home. Whatever we feel like."

Susan still looked unconvinced. "I mean, like what if I had an attack of appendicitis or somebody broke a leg or something?"

Their dad smiled. "Why? Don't you feel well?"

"I feel fine. I just wondered what if."

"Dork," Jim said. "Just try not to climb any big ladders for the next day or so."

"I suppose we *could* have accidents or get sick,"

said their dad, "but the chances are remote. There really isn't any need to worry."

"Then again," said Jim, "what if this runaway ax murderer came crawling out of a snowbank and tried to smash down our door and rip our throats out? I mean, you never know."

"Jimmy! Dad, will you tell him to knock it off?"

"Let's change the subject." Their mother offered the sack of marshmallows. "More?"

"Another thing," Susan said. "I'm really sick of having to use that stupid portable folding potty in the cabin."

"Then go outside," Jim said, smiling at his sister's scowling face.

That night, bundled in heavy blankets against the chill, Jim could hear the powerful wind. He shifted one way and then the other on his cot, but still he couldn't get away from the wind's high-pitched wail. As he listened, it seemed as though the wind grew in strength. "Great," he grumbled to himself. "Wind won't let you do anything during the day, and won't let you sleep at night."

In the morning, Jim awakened to the sound of his mother coughing. Her cold had become worse. Later, his dad cooked some hot, steaming oatmeal for everyone on the wood stove in the kitchen. "Another day or two at least," he said, nodding his head toward the door.

After breakfast Jim decided to put on his warmest

clothes and go outside to look around. When he opened the front door, he came face to face with a wall of snow that reached more than halfway up the door frame.

"Let's get at it," Jim's dad said, pulling on a goose-down jacket. He took a shovel from inside the door, tossed it toward Jim and then picked up another for himself.

Pushing into the waist-high snow, they managed to get out far enough to get the door shut behind them. Then, working slowly and steadily, they began to clear a deep, tunnel-like trench outward, away from the cabin. "At least let's clear a way to the wood-pile," said Jim's dad, "and another one over there to the 'necessary house.'" It was Jim's parents' term for the little outdoor toilet that sat at the edge of the trees.

"Be nice to get back where they have real bath-rooms," Jim mumbled as he shoveled.

Within half an hour they had reached the wood-pile—or what was left of it.

"Gee," Jim said, scraping snow from the remaining logs. "We used up more wood than I thought—just since yesterday."

"Still, enough for a day or so," said his dad. "Let's take in what's left."

"Can't even see where the trail to the valley is." Jim banged his mittens together to knock off some of the snow.

"Doesn't matter," said his dad. "We sure as heck can't drive anywhere."

When they reentered the cabin, Jim could hear his mother coughing even before they opened the door. She was seated by the fire, bundled in a blanket.

"When we get out," Jim's dad said, "first thing we'll do is see a doctor and get you something for that cough."

That night Jim got irritated all over again when he heard the wind. It screamed and groaned and whooshed! and moaned for hours into the night. As morning approached, it seemed that he had just barely gotten to sleep when he was awakened by a horrendous roar, a rolling, thunderous boom! outside, punctuated by the crackle and crunch of trees and limbs breaking.

"What the heck was that?" Jim shouted as he sat bolt upright on the cot. The roar and crackling continued at a distance until the sound faded, leaving only the whistling wind whirling about the cabin.

Jim's dad, pulling at his pants and heavy wool shirt, ran from the back bedroom. Jim already had his pants and shirt partway on. "Let's take a look," said his dad, grabbing his jacket and tossing Jim's jacket toward him.

Outside, the night wind had half-filled the trenches they had dug the day before. Rushing outward, they both were shocked when they reached the end of the path and looked over across the steep, narrow ravine toward the Wilsons' cabin. The distance, straight across, was less than a half-mile, but the ravine was more than 100 feet deep and filled with snow. Where the cabin had stood was now a massive mound of white, dotted like a porcupine with broken trees and branches. More trees and branches lay in a sweeping path that continued on down the mountain slope toward the valley and the lodge below.

"Oh, no . . ." Jim's father exhaled slowly, squinting in the direction of the valley. "Avalanche."

Jim was startled. *"Avalanche?* What about the Wilsons?"

"I don't know."

"Do you think they're dead?"

His dad sounded exasperated. "I don't *know*, Jim. Right now, I have to worry about *us*. It could happen again, and this time it could come down on our side."

"So what do we do?"

"Not much choice. We stay put, and hope somebody reaches us. People know there are cabins up here, and sooner or later somebody will try and get through. We just don't know when." His tone changed. "Listen, Jim. Don't say anything to your mother or to Susan, but we have a little problem here. We don't have enough wood for more than a day, and your mom is a lot more sick than I thought. We'll have to keep bundled up with lots of clothing, keep the smallest fire we possibly can, and try to stay calm. That's where you come in. No disaster jokes or horror stories. And don't mention the Wilsons. This situation is far more serious than we realized."

Looking around at the massive mounds of drifting snow, now almost covering their cabin, Jim felt a knot of dread in the pit of his stomach. For all they knew, the Wilsons could be lying dead and frozen in the smashed remains of their cabin. And the way the snow had continued to fill in, it could be several days—*maybe a week or more*—before anyone could get up here from the valley floor to rescue them.

"Did you find out what that noise was?" Susan asked when they reentered the cabin. She was bundled up in her favorite chair with a blanket wrapped around her.

"Buncha snow rolling down the valley," Jim said. "Nothing to worry about."

"Think I'll try and make our wood last a little longer," Jim's dad said, sounding surprisingly calm and matter-of-fact. "I suggest we all put on our skier's underwear, wool socks, sweaters, down jackets, and so forth, even inside here, so we can stay warm with a little less fire. Especially you, Ruth." He patted Jim's mother on the shoulder. She was seated near the fire and she, too, had a blanket wrapped around her.

When they had all put on their outdoor clothing and were huddled near the fireplace, Jim's dad said, "Well, what should we do? Tell stories?"

"Tell us about when you were in Viet Nam," Jim said.

"Naw, why don't we talk about something happy or funny?" his dad said. "Like the time Jim managed to start the car and ended up driving through Mrs. Olansky's backyard and garden. What were you? About five years old?"

Jim and Susan smiled, but their mother remained serious. "I'm worried," she said, and coughed again. "We're in trouble here, aren't we?" She stared at Jim's dad.

"I think we're okay," he said softly. "It's not going to help to worry. Let's head for bed early tonight, and bundle up nice and warm."

That night Jim could barely sleep, listening intently for that same horrible, telltale sound, the distant roar that might grow in seconds to a massive thunder as it brought tons of snow and trees and debris crashing down from the mountain on top of them . . . Instead, for hours he heard only the same mournful howl of the wind licking around the cabin walls like the tongue of a massive, hungry animal.

"Well, that's it," Susan said the next morning, holding up a bread wrapper with two slices remaining in the bottom. "The last of the food."

"It's not like we're at the end of the earth," Jim's dad said, forcing a smile. He took the bread out, tore it in pieces and handed it to the other three. "We'll still get rescued."

"Sure," Susan said, her eyes wide and fearful. "But when? And besides, the firewood's gone. What now?"

"We stay bundled up," their dad said. "I don't know what else to tell you. Maybe we can break up some chairs or something and burn them."

That afternoon, with the cold becoming severe inside the cabin, Jim and his dad were beginning to smash some of the front-room furniture for firewood when they heard the sound of a motor outside. They stopped for a moment, looking at each other in disbelief, then both raced to the door and threw it open. Outside on a mound of snow near the end of the pathway—now drifted nearly full—stood a diamond-bright, custom black van with polished chrome wheel covers, wide tires, chrome exhausts, and smoke-tinted glass all around. It was just the kind of van Jim had dreamed of owning some day, after he had his driver's license.

Already wading from the van toward the cabin was a tall, pleasant-looking man. He wore high boots, a long, dark parka trimmed in wolf fur, and shiny aviator sunglasses that reflected the light off the drifts of snow.

"Hello, there," the man called out, smiling. "Thought you folks could use a lift down the mountain. Avalanche made it pretty rough getting in and out of here last few days." As he approached Jim and his dad, the man took off his sunglasses and put out his hand.

Jim's dad shook hands without speaking.

"Boy, are we glad to see you," Jim said, smiling and holding the door open for them to walk inside. "We're out of food, and the wood just ran out."

"I can only step in for a minute," the man said. "Managed to get your neighbors, the Wilsons, out after they got half-buried by the avalanche."

"Avalanche! Oh, I'm so glad you got them," Jim's mother said between coughs.

"Well, I managed to get around to a place or two today," said the man. "Plenty of folks in trouble, just like you. Not too bad, though, once you get down the mountain a ways. People are saying now the weather's supposed to lighten up a bit during the coming week."

"You with the sheriff's department or something?" Jim asked.

"No," the man said, smiling again. "Just like to help out at times like this. I've had a lot of experience."

"Sorry we can't offer you any coffee or anything . . ." Jim's mom said, clearing her throat.

"No problem," said the man. "I understand. Well, shall we go? I'm sure you folks would enjoy a hot meal and a bath and a good night's sleep at the lodge in the valley."

"How on earth did you get up here?" Jim's mother asked, pulling the blanket tighter around her.

"Great van out there," the man said, still smiling. "Goes through anything. Plus, getting around on these trails depends a lot on driver know-how. I've been getting around in this stuff for a long time."

"Isn't this great?" said Susan, hopping up and down from the cold. "At least tonight we can get a nice—*warm*—night's sleep. And I can't *wait* to order a huge breakfast at the lodge in the morning. I'm gonna have two of everything."

The man laughed, showing white, nearly perfect teeth. He nodded in Susan's direction. "So, what do you say? Shall we head down to the lodge before it starts to get dark?"

"I appreciate it, Mister," said Jim's dad slowly, looking at Susan and Jim and then back at the man. "That's a generous offer and it sounds wonderful, but I think we'll stay here for the night. We shouldn't have any problem, and we can decide tomorrow what to do."

"*Dad!*" Susan shrieked, staring at him. She turned to her mother and held her mittened hands palms-up, questioning.

"Are you *sure* . . . ?" Jim's mom began, looking at Jim's dad. "I mean, we *could* be in the lodge before nightfall."

"It's up to you," the man said. "You do what you want. You're sure welcome, though, if you want to go."

"Dad?" Susan said again, her eyes filling with tears.

"No, we'll stay," Jim's dad said, in a tone that

meant the issue was closed. "Thanks just the same."

After the man had waved and left and they heard the van move away through the snow, Jim turned to his dad. "Dad, why would you . . ."

His dad only waved him silent and stood for a long time, staring at the fireplace. Susan huddled in a corner, crying softly, the blanket still pulled tightly around her. Their mother sat silently in another corner, staring absently at the door.

"I have to do what I think is right," Jim's dad said finally. "Let's get the rest of this furniture broken up."

That night, as all four of them lay huddled against each other beside the tiny flame in the fireplace, Jim couldn't rid himself of his anger. He *could* have been relaxing right now in a soft bed in the lodge with a full supper in his stomach. Instead, he was lying on the stupid floor in a nearly frozen cabin. All because his dad refused help from a stranger.

The stranger had seemed like a pretty sharp guy. And the van was incredible. But now they had to put up with another night without enough heat, without food, and who knows? Maybe another avalanche.

The next day they got up without speaking and pulled the blankets more tightly around them to keep warm. "I guess the rest of the furniture goes," Jim's dad finally said. He tipped up the kitchen table, knocked the legs off and began to smash the tabletop into pieces small enough to fit in the fireplace.

Jim was still too angry to speak. Susan was upset,

too. It was easy to tell. She just huddled in one corner, scowling and staring at the fireplace.

Their dad got a small fire going with the table wood. Although no one said anything, they all seemed to be thinking the same thing Jim was thinking: there's only one chair left to break and burn. Then what do we do?

After the fire had burned a while, Jim thought he heard another noise outside. He strained to hear, but the growing wind blocked out any other sound. He leaned back against one wall and strained to hear. Within minutes he heard it again, and this time there was no mistaking it. The sharp, low-pitched whine of a snowmobile engine was moving closer, rising and falling as it cut through the deep snowdrifts.

"Hey!" Jim and Susan said together, jumping to their feet. Their dad and mom jumped up, too, and all four raced to the cabin door. Throwing it open, they saw a man seated on a snowmobile that had a large Sheriff's Department insignia on the side. The machine's wide track and front skis were barely visible in the soft snow. The deputy waved and got off the machine, leaving it on the drift where he stopped.

"Everyone all right in there?" he called, as another deputy on a snowmobile and then four or five others roared into view.

Jim's dad nodded and motioned the deputy into the cabin.

"Worst I've seen in years," said the officer, shaking

some of the snow off his heavy, insulated parka. "We got drifts out there twelve, fifteen feet high. And your neighbors over there . . . I don't know if you knew."

"Knew what?" said Jim's dad, staring at the deputy.

"The Wilsons," said the deputy. "In that cabin across the gulch. They didn't make it. Avalanche took the cabin and killed all three. Terrible thing."

"We wondered about them," said Jim's dad. "We saw the avalanche path after it went down the mountain. "That's awful. That's just awful."

"Wait a minute . . ." Jim started to say. He felt the hair on the back of his neck beginning to rise. His dad waved him quiet.

"Well, we're gonna get you folks out," said the officer, as two of the deputies pushed the door open and stepped inside. "Even with snowmobiles it wasn't easy getting through this stuff."

"Coulda gone yesterday," said Susan, scowling at her dad.

"How's that?" asked the deputy.

"This guy came by," Susan said, glancing again at her dad, then back at the deputy. "Had this van and said he'd take us down."

"He had a *what?*" asked the deputy, squinting at Susan.

"Custom van, or van. Whatever you call them," Susan said.

"Yeah," Jim added. "Really nice. All shiny, with

chrome wheel covers, wide tires, chrome pipes, smoked glass. Said he was pretty good at driving in this snow. Said he managed to get to the Wilsons. That's what I don't understand.''

The deputy hesitated, glancing first at the other two officers, then back at Susan and Jim. Finally, he looked at Jim and Susan's dad. ''Did you see this van, too?''

Jim's dad didn't answer the question, and Jim noticed he had a strange expression.

''I guess I don't know who or what you saw,'' said the deputy, ''but it couldn't have been anything with wheels. A lot of drifts along the trail are higher than two-story houses, and there's simply nothing on wheels that could have made it up here. Absolutely nothing. Our *snowmobiles* had a tough time getting here—and they're on *skis!*''

Jim couldn't figure it out. And his dad still hadn't said anything. ''Dad . . . ?'' he asked. ''What about the guy?''

''Don't want to talk about it,'' Jim's dad said. ''Let's just go with these officers.''

''I'm curious, too,'' Jim's mother said, staring at Jim's dad. ''We wanted to go yesterday, but for some reason . . .''

Jim's dad sighed. ''I thought I knew who he was.'' He spoke softly and looked away from them, as though staring into the distance. ''I thought I might have seen him before, but I wasn't so sure. Now I'm sure.''

"Well, *who*, then?" said Susan, still scowling.

Her dad's eyes still were focused on some distant point, some place the rest couldn't see. His voice was softer still, now almost a whisper. "It was a long time ago. I saw him more than once, in the war."

Now everyone was staring at him.

"I've seen him before," he said again softly. "His name is Death."

Sarah's Locket

Afternoon sunlight danced on the crystal surfaces of the bedroom lamp, leaving bright, tiny rainbows that seemed to hover in the air near Sarah's hands. Looking through the drawer in the night table near her mother's bed, Sarah was amazed as always at all the souvenirs her mother kept in the table: school art projects Sarah had brought home, dating back to first and second grade; reports and notes from teachers; snapshots of Sarah and her brother, Mark, and parents on vacation; old letters; odds and ends . . . and school pictures.

Whenever Sarah needed a school picture to exchange with a friend—as she did today—she knew the likeliest spot to find one would be in this drawer.

"Find the picture yet?" her mother called from the kitchen downstairs.

"Not yet," said Sarah. "I'm still looking."

"Try over on the right side. You might find a few wallet-size photos left at the bottom of the drawer."

Sarah hadn't told her mother why she needed the

picture. She smiled as she thought of it. Her friend, Sandy, knew this cute new boy in eighth grade, and he'd told Sandy he liked Sarah and would like to get a picture of her—without her knowing about it, of course. Sarah smiled again when she thought about how "secret" the whole thing was.

Poking through the bits and scraps of paper, she finally spotted six or seven of her newest class pictures, all printed together on one sheet. Now she'd have to find a pair of scissors. Maybe her mom had scissors in here, too. Otherwise she'd have to get a pair out of the kitchen.

Lifting more papers out of the way, she uncovered something she'd never seen in the drawer before. It was a small, silver, almost-square locket with a tiny, fragile-looking chain still attached. The locket was partially wrapped in old tissue paper, some of which had been torn away.

The outside of the case was scratched and worn, and looked very old. Lifting it and turning it over, Sarah saw almost-invisible initials etched on the back in tiny, sweeping letters.

Placing it in the palm of one hand, she gently pressed the latch and opened the cover. Inside was an old-fashioned, brown-toned photo of a young woman who looked as though she might have been no more than a few years older than Sarah when the photograph was taken. The woman wore a high-necked blouse with frilly lace around the collar. Her long brown hair was pulled up and pinned high on her head. She was pretty, with high, graceful cheek-bones and gentle, delicate features.

Sarah stared at the woman's eyes for several moments. They seemed so warm and kind. It was as though she had been talking quietly with a friend, and had simply stopped for a moment as the picture was taken.

"Mom?" Sarah called as she skipped downstairs. "Who's this?" She held the locket in the sunlight in the kitchen for her mother to see. Sarah's fifteen-year-old brother, Mark, got up from the kitchen table where he was munching on crackers and came close.

"Oh, my, I don't even know," her mother said, squinting at the locket. "I found that in the attic a while back and put it in my drawer. I got it years ago from our old neighbor, Miss Beale. She just felt she wanted to give me something once when I helped her trim her rose bushes. Miss Beale was very old at the time. She was a bit eccentric and kept to herself, so some people around here told stories about her."

"Hey," Mark said, his eyes lighting up. "What kind of stories?"

"Foolishness. How she was strange, and had special powers. The usual silliness. The truth was, she was always nice to me. She said she gave me the locket simply because she had no use for it."

Her mother turned and continued cutting apples for a pie she was making. Soon she stopped and looked again at the locket, still nestled in Sarah's hand. "Interesting," she said. "Now that I think of it, I remember Miss Beale saying that the picture was of her great-grandmother, who died in a flu epidemic just after the Civil War. I guess the young woman was little more than a teenager when she died. She had a small baby at the time, who turned out to be Miss Beale's grandmother."

"Why didn't Miss Beale keep it?" Sarah asked, staring at the gentle eyes of the woman in the picture.

"Well, she was very old, and there was no one to give the locket to. Miss Beale had no family. She always said it was a shame about her great-grandmother. All the others in their family lived nice, long lives, but that young woman never had a chance."

"It *is* sad," Sarah said.

Her mother resumed cutting apples. "Miss Beale was gone in less than a year after she gave me the locket. If you wish, you can have it. I don't have any need for a locket, either."

"I'm going to look for a place where no one will find it," Sarah said. "Seems sad. This is all that's left of this person. All that's left in the whole world."

Sarah immediately went to her room, where she looked for a special place to put the locket. Finally she decided to keep it in the back of the deepest, most out-of-the-way shelf in her closet. She decided, too, that she'd never show it to anyone, not even her closest friends.

The next day, Sarah couldn't help taking out the locket again and just staring at it. The woman in the picture had such pretty hair and perfect skin. Sarah wondered if Miss Beale had ever stared at the picture, too, and if she had wondered, as Sarah did, what the silent, pleasant-looking young woman had been like.

During the next few weeks, she left the locket hidden in her closet and didn't take it out at all—although she finally couldn't resist telling her best friend, Sandy.

"My mom had a locket once, too," Sandy said. "It had a picture of my dad in it, in his Army uniform. I think she lost it, or maybe not. I don't know. I haven't seen it for a long time."

When Sandy asked to see the locket, Sarah said she'd show it to her sometime, but not right now. "I hide it way back in my closet," she said, breaking her promise to herself never to tell anyone where it was hidden. "If you tell, I'll absolutely, positively never tell you anything again."

"Sometime I'd like to see it," Sandy said. "Old stuff like that is kind of interesting."

"Miss Beale said the woman in the picture died real young," Sarah said. "She never got to be old."

One Saturday afternoon, while Sarah's mother was out buying groceries, Sarah made certain no one else was around, then she took the locket out and sat down on the chair in her room. Holding it to the light so she could see, she stared again at the young woman's face. For several minutes, she scarcely breathed, studying the face and especially the eyes. They seemed to reach out to her from across so many years. They were haunting, almost. They drew her closer, and seemed so much more than a simple photograph.

What were you like? Sarah asked softly. Did you laugh? Did you cry? Did you have hopes and dreams and secrets? Were you happy when you got married? Did you sing to your baby, and hold her close? What was life like so very many years ago?

Still, the young lady in the locket just looked out the same pleasant way, with the same relaxed, kindly expression.

I wish I could have known you, Sarah said. It's so sad you got cheated out of life.

After she had placed the locket at the back of the shelf again, Sarah walked downstairs, found a soda in the refrigerator and wandered out to the front step. As she sat there, watching old Mr. Dykstra across the street trim his hedge, the image in the locket kept coming back to her.

There certainly were trees and grass and hedges and flowers when you were around, Sarah said softly. Did you enjoy walking in the grass? Did you grow flowers? I'll bet life was more peaceful back then without cars and jets and television.

In the weeks that followed, she felt more and more drawn to the locket. It was fascinating, and a little scary, too, the way she couldn't seem to leave it alone.

She was developing a whole new interest in the world of the last century. Sarah pestered her mother until her mother gave in and took her to the library downtown, where the librarian helped her find several books about life just after the Civil War.

She laughed at whalebone corsets and high-button shoes, and the "bustles" that women wore to make their long dresses stick out in the back. She found pictures of horse-drawn buggies and kerosene lamps and special coffee cups with extra little "bridges" built in to keep men's bushy handlebar moustaches out of their coffee. Men wore shirts with stiff, removable collars, and children wore funny-looking shoes with buttons on the side. And people never seemed to smile in pictures.

"I think you're spending more time than you should, looking at old books and pictures," Sarah's mother said more than once. "My goodness! You spend more time doing that than you spend on your homework!"

"It's so interesting, Mom," is all Sarah would say. She looked for more books and pictures. And every few days she just *had* to take out the locket again and stare at the silent face inside.

One day while she was sitting alone in her room, studying the face again, something very strange occurred. She distinctly heard the jingling of a harness and the steady clip-clop of horses' hooves. She ran to the window and looked out, but saw only old Mr. Dykstra's car, parked where he always parked it. As the sound grew louder, she heard mixed with it the groan and clatter of a wooden wagon, the short yips! and whoas! of a team driver and other, more distant sounds of horses, wagons, and people.

"I think you're right, Mom," she said when her mother came in later to say good-night. "I think I've looked at too many books. Today I swear I heard horses and wagons."

"Now maybe you'll listen to me," her mother said, smiling.

Although she tried as hard as she could, Sarah simply couldn't leave the locket alone for more than a few days at a time. And nearly every time now, something strange and weird seemed to happen. She didn't tell her mother anymore, because she was afraid her mother would take away the locket and she would never see it again.

More and more, she heard the sounds of horses and wagons, people talking in rural, western drawls, babies crying, and the tapping rhythm of hard heels on wooden sidewalks. Often, as though in a dream, she heard the faint voices of young men and women, sometimes talking, sometimes laughing.

She was worried now, because it seemed as though it was becoming harder and harder to tell the difference between the shadowy, dream sounds associated with the locket and the real sounds of the world around her. Still, she returned again and again to her room, trying to do so when her parents wouldn't notice. Each time she heard the echoing dream sounds: people talking and laughing, fiddle music, wood crackling on fires, thunder, the hiss of rain, the roar of mammoth grass fires, and the panicked shouts ("Get the animals out of the barn!").

Now she was beginning to get other sensory impressions as well. Seated in her chair by the window in her room, she smelled the scents of fresh-turned rich earth, of new-mown hay and alfalfa grass, horses and harness leather, baking bread and pipe tobacco and sweet clover and homemade lye soap. Sometimes her vision clouded, and she saw bolts of brightly colored calico cloth, muddy streets, ladies in broad-brimmed hats, cracker barrels, and jars filled with penny candy.

Sarah was beginning to feel almost at home with the strange and interesting parade of images, scents, and sounds that continued to surround her whenever the locket was near. She knew she shouldn't spend quite so much time in the world of the past. In spite of herself, though, she actually looked forward to the times when she could sit for a few minutes in her room alone and feel the world that had seemed so distant and yet now seemed so familiar. It was as if the woman in the locket had almost become her best friend.

"Can I see that locket?" her friend Sandy said one Friday after school. "The one old Miss Beale gave your mom from a long time ago?"

"I guess," Sarah said, already sorry that she'd agreed. She and Sandy went up the stairs to Sarah's room. Sarah made certain no one else was upstairs before she closed the door.

Sandy plopped onto the end of Sarah's bed and tossed her book bag onto the floor. "Why are you so careful?" she asked.

"I don't know," Sarah said. "That locket is special, and I just don't want anything to happen to it." She lifted the locket from its hidden spot and placed it in Sandy's hand.

Sandy studied the old photo. "Funny, isn't it?" she said. "This old picture's nothing but an image on paper. The real person's been in her grave for more than a hundred years. Now she's just dust, a few bones, a little hair, and a few bits of cloth."

"That sounds terrible," Sarah said.

Sandy shrugged. "In the picture she's pretty forever."

Sarah was tempted to tell Sandy about all the sights and smells and sounds associated with the locket, but Sandy would probably think she was ready for the loony bin. She just took the locket and placed it back in its hiding place.

"Gotta go," Sandy said, grabbing her book bag and heading for the door. "I'll call you later. Maybe we can play a little tennis."

When Sandy had gone, Sarah lay down on her bed and stared at the ceiling. She was tired, but she felt restless and a little jumpy, too. She tried to think of anything *other* than the locket. She tried to remember the last time she and Sandy had played tennis, how Sandy had hit a ball out of the court and nearly beaned an old man sitting on a park bench. She thought of parties she had gone to in the last year, of boys she liked and of the trip to the mountains her family was planning for late summer.

Still, try as she might, she couldn't keep her mind away from the locket for long. She kept seeing the woman's face with its perfect skin, and with no mole like the one Sarah had on her cheek. She kept seeing the woman's beautiful, silky-dark hair that wasn't sun-bleached and blonde like Sarah's.

Now, the other impressions began coming back, too—the sounds of horses and wagons, louder than ever, and heel taps on wooden sidewalks; the yips! and whoas! of wagon-team drivers and the groan of wagon wheels on muddy, rutted paths; the faint tinkle of saloon music and the echoing voices rising and falling in a kaleidoscope of words and laughter.

She wished that it would all stop. She wanted to rest, to think about something else. She put her fingers in her ears to try and block the sounds, but it was no use. She began to feel a rising sense of panic, as though her mind were coming apart. The pull of the ages, of time long past, became stronger and stronger, changing her world from a pleasant place of comfort to a threatening corridor of fear, a place where unknown forces were trying to drag her into gaping and ominous shadows. She wanted to scream, to tell the images to stop, but the sound of her own voice caught in her throat. She felt herself thrashing about on her bed as the sounds and the smells and the sights continued to swirl about her like insistent hands, dragging and pulling at her.

Clapping her hands to the sides of her head, Sarah leaped from the bed, rushed to the closet and snatched the locket from the back shelf. She had to get it away from here, once and for all. Her mother had gotten it from the old woman; she would ask her mother to give it away or smash it.

She raced for the stairs and started down. Her ears were pounding and she felt light-headed. Halfway down the stairs she spotted her mother and Mark, talking quietly at the kitchen table. Now Sarah felt she might faint, right there on the stairs. She paused, gripping the handrail, and opened her mouth to call for help, but no sound came out.

Catching her breath, she looked down and was gripped by horror. Her feet and ankles already had turned to bleached-white, dusty bone, and now the flesh was disappearing from her legs and arms as well. She opened her mouth again to scream, to shriek, but the sound that came out seemed to echo down some filmy, vaporous corridor beyond her mother and Mark. How could they not hear her? With a final effort, Sarah raised a bone-white arm and flung the locket in the direction of her mother.

Finishing the last of her coffee, Sarah's mother rose

from the kitchen chair, turned toward the cupboard, then back to Mark. "Maybe Chinese food for dinner," she said cheerily.

"Sounds great," Mark said, pushing away from the table.

Spotting a small, shiny object on the floor in the corner, near the door to the kitchen, Sarah's mother reached over to pick it up. "I'll be darned," she said. "Here's that old locket that Sarah thought was so interesting. Bet she wonders where it is."

"Sarah?" her mother called, starting up the stairs. "Sarah? I found that old locket on the floor downstairs. Sarah?"

In the bedroom her mother found the bed slightly rumpled and the usual pieces of clothing scattered about the floor, but no sign of Sarah. "Funny," she mumbled. "I didn't see her leave with Sandy."

A curious, prickling sense of fear was beginning in a far corner of her consciousness. She walked back to the top of the stairs and called out. "Mark, have you seen Sarah? Did she go out?"

"Haven't seen her," came the reply.

Sarah's mother shrugged. She walked back into Sarah's room, then paused and stared again at the locket in the palm of her hand. Casually, almost absently, she pressed the delicate snap on the locket, opened the cover, and held the locket higher in the light from the window. She blinked, held the locket more directly in the sunlight and stared at it again closely, gasping in horror as she did so.

The photograph, brown-toned and clearly very old, was of Sarah, right down to the mole on her cheek. Her light golden hair was swept back high on her head, and she wore a high-necked, lace-trimmed blouse. Her expression was relaxed and pleasant, as though she had been talking to a friend and had merely paused a moment while the photograph was taken.

Sarah's mother stifled a scream. The locket seemed to possess an energy all its own. She dropped it on the bed and rushed from the room. "Sarah!" she called, almost tumbling down the stairs. *"Sarah!"*

Behind her, in Sarah's room, the locket remained on the bed where she'd dropped it. Although Sarah's mother was too far away now to hear, soft, distant sounds continued to echo around and over the worn silver surfaces and the photo inside. The sounds—tiny, fragmented, rising and falling—were those of horses, wagons, hard heels on wooden sidewalks, and over it all a sprinkling of voices and distant laughter . . .

Deadly Warm

If it weren't for Dr. Corbin's laboratory, Billy thought, I might never have a chance to get a new mountain bike.

Almost hidden in the rock-strewn, sandy hills a mile or so from Billy's house, the small, earth-colored laboratory had been there as long as Billy could remember. It looked lonely and forgotten, with just one door and no windows. The desert washes between Billy's house and the laboratory were choked with dense creosote brush, rangy mesquite, chaparral, and somber cactus, all lying in the distant shadows of the Santa Catalina range.

In the surrounding mountains, rising from the great Arizona desert, the legendary Apache and other Native Americans once had hunted and each day had watched the sun bleed color like splashes of paint across the stark, cloudless sky. Now there were roads and cars and a few towns. On the larger highways there were always tourists and truckers heading into, or out of, places like Tucson, only a few miles away, or Phoenix farther to the north.

The tiny house in which Billy lived with his mother and stepfather sat on the flats near a dusty road a half-mile from the highway. On days when he had found work, Billy's stepfather got up at 5:00 A.M. and drove his rusted pickup truck down the road to the highway, and from there went to construction sites around Tucson.

His stepfather was a large and powerful man, with blunt, work-hardened hands and thick shoulder and arm muscles built up from years of lifting and carrying boards and cement and concrete blocks on the job.

Sometimes he came back home in time for supper, and some days he didn't come home for hours. When he did come home on those days, he often smelled of different mixtures of things, of food and booze and stale smoke and sometimes perfume. And often on those days he was angry and quarrelsome, sometimes going so far as to hit Billy's mother and make her cry. If Billy's father were still alive, Billy was sure he wouldn't have acted that way.

To get away, Billy liked to wander along the dry washes and the hills, where his only companions were the wind, the hard, flat sun, and an occasional lizard.

The first year that he had ventured any distance away from the house, leaving the yelling and the crying and the pain behind, he had poked around with a stick in a dense mesquite thicket not far from a large saguaro cactus. When he did so, he had found one of the desert's most feared residents. Coiled on a flat rock partly covered by the mesquite, soaking up the warmth of the midday sun, had been a diamondback rattlesnake, sleek and fat and easily more than four feet long.

The snake had not struck at the stick, but instead had crawled away on the warm desert floor, raising its head and rattling a little as it moved—as if to say, I'm leaving because I'm not in a mood to fight right now, but don't ever think I'm afraid of you.

Billy had been so surprised he had dropped the stick. By the time he picked it up again, the snake had disappeared.

Later he had found another rattler, dead. He had cut the rattle off with his pocket knife and had taken it home to show his mother and stepfather. This nearly earned him a whipping.

"No snakes and no rattles," his stepfather had said, anger and nervousness sounding in his voice. "I pretty near died from one once. Caught me above the boot. They're dirty devils. I ain't afraid of nothin' on two legs, but I won't have any part of those things in my house."

Staring at him, Billy had seen genuine fear in his eyes, although the man tried to hide it. It seemed almost funny, in a way. All Billy held in his hand were the harmless rattles from a dead snake, but those rattles worried a man of great size and strength.

After that, although Billy had looked for more snakes and for rattles when he walked in the desert, he hadn't said anything about it. He still found it curious that something as harmless as the rattles from a dead snake could have such a surprising effect on his stepfather.

Billy thought of this often as he rode the bus to the middle school he attended at the edge of Tucson. The school library had only a couple of books on snakes, but from these he began to learn about the rattlers, to see where they lived, why they behaved as they did, and why they should be a source of such fear and so many folktales. He also learned the differences between diamondback rattlers and the Mojave rattlers that could be found nearby.

Sometimes on weekends his cousin, Raul, whose hobby was snakes, came and stayed with Billy, and sometimes he went to Raul's house. From Raul, who lived farther to the west near the Sierra Pinta range, he learned about Sonoran Desert sidewinders and black-tailed rattlers. Raul's father had told him how the sidewinder makes the curious pattern of "steps" over sand that gives it its name, and how snakes, being cold-blooded, look for warm places and like to bask in the sun when the ground and the rocks are not too cool or too hot.

Raul's father also told Raul about the size and spirit

of the diamondbacks, how stories were told of snakes more than six feet long, weighing more than twenty pounds, and how the diamondback was known to be a fierce and dangerous fighter.

He told him, too, many stories and legends—mostly untrue, Billy suspected—about how this or that rattler had "charmed" a rabbit, a frog, or even a person merely by fixing the victim with its hypnotic gaze, then sinking its fangs into the hapless victim's flesh.

In learning about snakes, Billy had learned something else. People sometimes will pay money for good specimens. When he had inquired at the dusty little laboratory near the highway, he had met Dr. Corbin, and he had found that the laboratory director was conducting research for the University of Arizona on substances found in snake venom. In this research he needed snakes. Dr. Corbin had offered a deal: He would buy any rattlers Billy could bring in for a dollar apiece, and for larger diamondbacks he would pay three dollars. The arrangement would continue until Dr. Corbin didn't need any more snakes.

Billy decided he would save his snake money until he could buy a new mountain bike, a rugged ten-speed with wide, knobby tires. He had seen exactly the one he wanted when he had gone to Tucson with his mother and stepfather to buy groceries.

Now, after school, whenever he could, he went poking about the country near his house, looking among cactus and mesquite for diamondbacks and

Mojave rattlers. Many times he found nothing, but sometimes he got lucky. The hunting always was best in the spring months. The snakes were most active then, before the blistering heat of summer forced them to seek shelter each day and come out only after the sun was down.

When Raul came to visit, he learned from him how to use a long, forked stick to hold the snakes and keep them at a safe distance until he could flip them into a wooden box made from scrap lumber. He had punched many tiny holes in the box for air, but even so, he had to hurry to the laboratory each time he found a rattler, so that it would not die from the heat.

Billy's mother and stepfather knew of his new interest in snakes. His mother said it was too dangerous and she wished he would stop. His stepfather only said that no snakes ever would be allowed near their house.

Not many days after, Billy heard his stepfather come home late again, and he heard the two of them arguing about him. When he saw his stepfather strike his mother, and heard her cry out again, he screamed at the man to stop. This time, the man chased him more than half a mile into the night until his stepfather gave up and returned to the house. Finally Billy went back to the house, too, and Billy's mother got his stepfather to promise he wouldn't hurt Billy.

Each time Raul came to visit, it was fun talking and poking about in the tangled bushes and laughing together. Raul knew more about snakes than anyone Billy had ever met.

"Some people even say the roadrunner knows how to kill rattlers," Raul said. "He's only a foolish bird, but they say he knows."

"I don't believe it," Billy said. "*Birds* killing *rattlesnakes?* It sounds crazy to me."

"Some people say roadrunners know, and so do coyotes," Raul said. "I don't know if it's true, but they say coyotes and roadrunners sometimes stay between the rattler and the shade of bushes on a hot day, challenging and fighting and wearing out the rattler until he dies from the hot sun. The snake can't sweat, so he dies very quickly."

"I still doubt it," Billy said to his smiling cousin.

One Saturday evening, after an especially good hunt that yielded three good diamondbacks and two Mojave rattlers, Billy hurried with his wooden box to Dr. Corbin's laboratory. The desert temperature was dropping rapidly and a cold, dry chill was settling over the ground. Although Dr. Corbin usually was in the laboratory on Saturdays, this time Billy found a sign that said, "Closed. Back Monday A.M."

Now what do I do with my snakes? Billy thought. I worked too hard hunting them to just turn them loose. And if I leave them here, they'll be dead in a day for sure.

He thought about it for a moment, and decided to take a risk: If he took the box home, he might be able to hide it from his stepfather and keep it cool for a couple of days, and then he could go and collect from Dr. Corbin.

Walking along the path to the house, he heard his mother scream just as the house came into view. When he heard her scream again, it made his blood run cold and he began to run, trying not to drop the box, now unusually heavy with his snakes inside. With the bouncing and running, several of the snakes began to rattle.

The rusted pickup truck sat near the door to the house, with the driver's-side door half-open. Approaching the truck, Billy reached out and felt the heat coming off the hood above the engine. The heat felt good against the growing night chill. The warmth of the engine meant his stepfather had just come home.

More worried than ever, his hands trembling, Billy placed the wooden box on the hood of the truck and crept inside the house. At first there was no sound, and then he heard the slow, whimpering cry of his mother coming from the tiny living room. The light was not on in the room, but he saw her there, seated in one corner of the worn sofa. Sometimes she sat there to watch the family's small, black-and-white television set that rested on the metal cart in the other corner of the room. Now she simply sat in the shadows, crying.

Before Billy could speak, she raised her hand and

waved him away. "Please go to your room, and just stay there," she whispered, her voice catching a little as she spoke. "Everything will be all right."

"Where is he?" Billy said, his own voice a half-whisper.

She hesitated, then nodded in the direction of their bedroom, on the opposite side of the wall behind her.

"What's wrong?" Billy said, moving closer.

"Please!" she whispered, louder. "Please, just go to your room."

Billy hesitated, anxious not to disobey and make her feel worse. But he couldn't resist moving closer, straining to see in the shadows. Something didn't seem right in the way she crossed and uncrossed her arms, and kept touching her cheek with one hand.

As he leaned close, she began to cry again, and Billy saw that one eye was terribly swollen and her nose had streaks of smeared blood around the nostrils. Blood and tears were smeared together on her cheeks. Her hand was trembling as she raised it to shield her face from his vision.

"Will you *please* go to your room?" she asked again, turning away from him. "I told you, things will be all right."

"Did he do this?" Billy asked, thinking immediately that it was a dumb question, since it was obvious that he had.

"Sometimes," she said, her voice still wavering, "when he has been to town and has drunk too much he gets a little crazy, but I don't think he really means to hurt me. I just don't want you to have any trouble with him. That's why I want you to go to your room.''

Billy turned from her, but instead of going to his own room, he stepped inside the other bedroom. The light was on, and his stepfather, fully clothed, was sprawled on the bed, already snoring loudly. His feet, laced into heavy, work-worn boots, hung over the end of the bed. His hands, flopped open and palms-up, reached each side.

The sight of him, and the knowledge of what he had done, made Billy so angry he could scarcely contain himself. He could feel that his face was flushed and sweaty. And he kept seeing his mother's face and hearing the sound of her cry.

He stood there for several minutes, not sure what to do, hating this man who had hurt his mother so often. All he could think about was the sound of his mother weeping and the marks on her face. Slowly, surely, it came to him that he must do something. Whatever it takes, he said to himself, I want him to remember this time. I want him to know that one person just can't do these things to another person.

Quietly, his heart beating faster, he stepped to the window and raised it high, letting in the sharp, cold air off the desert. Then he took down a blanket from the closet shelf and placed it over the sleeping man, gently tucking it in and around him and making sure it covered his feet also.

Moving out of the bedroom, he peered into the living room and saw that his mother was resting with her eyes closed and her head against the back of the sofa. He could see that her breath still caught a little every few moments, the last remnants of weeping.

Outside, the truck was cooling quickly. Billy grabbed the wooden box and tiptoed inside again, holding the box close and hoping that its occupants would make no noise.

After entering the bedroom, he stopped and watched once more, gripping the box close to him. The man hadn't moved. His chest still rose and fell with the slow rhythm of his breathing. The chill from the open window had now made the entire room cold.

Billy lifted the box and in a single, rapid motion, flipped open the cover and dumped the three diamondbacks and two Mojave rattlers onto the end of the bed. Then he closed the box and walked quickly from the room, closing the door behind him.

Lying down in his own bedroom without bothering to undress, he stared at the ceiling for what seemed a long time. All he heard was the gentle airflow of his own breathing. Finally he drifted into a shallow, fitful sleep.

When he awoke, he wondered if the entire night had passed. By the lighted dial of his clock, he saw that it was still an hour or more until dawn. He was lying there, wondering why he had awakened, when he heard a sharp, high-pitched yell from the far bedroom. Jumping up, he ran to the room and found his mother already there, standing in the open doorway and staring in the direction of the bed.

Her mouth was open, as though she intended to speak, but she was saying nothing. Billy's stepfather still lay on his back on the bed. The blanket with which Billy had covered him was partly pulled off of him and bunched in one of his hands. The five rattlers seemed to be slowly burrowing under and around him, between his knees, under his back and under his arms. He was rigid and his face was stone-white.

"Just don't move," Billy said, moving closer to the bed. "Snakes are deaf. They can't hear a thing. But they can feel movement."

His stepfather's eyes were wide and unblinking, and from the man's mouth came a strangled scream, but he struggled not to move his mouth or his eyes or any other part of him.

"Billy . . ." It was Billy's mother, speaking so low Billy could barely hear. "Billy . . . *please* . . . how do we get those away from him?" Her hands were trembling and her gaze was still fixed rigidly on the bed.

"Just don't move," Billy said again, moving still closer.

"Why . . . ?" Her question was directed at Billy, but she stared at the bed, her eyes wide with fear.

"Snakes go where it's warm," Billy said. "The bed was the warmest spot in this room." He was surprised at the sound of his own voice, how calm he sounded, almost matter-of-fact.

"Please, can you get them out of there, *please?*" She still stared, as though afraid to move or change her gaze.

"I don't know," Billy said. There was a certain satisfaction in seeing the expression of pure, unchecked horror on the man's face. "I'd say he'd better not even blink."

Now, from the man, came a tiny series of light whimpering sounds. From the look of him, he was even trying to avoid breathing any more than necessary.

Billy got the wooden box from his room and set it on the floor near his stepfather. Then he got the long, forked stick from where he'd left it out by the back door and gently, slowly, began to lift the snakes up and out and place them back in the box.

"What if the stick upsets them and they bite him?" Billy's mother asked in a half-whisper.

Billy only shrugged and continued to lift each snake off the bed. One of the diamondbacks twisted its head around and appeared to be trying to strike as it was lifted away, but the strike missed. Even so, the man's eyes grew wider and Billy heard him gasp, still without moving his mouth or eyes.

Finally Billy lifted the last snake, a Mojave rattler, away from the man and dropped it into the box. Flipping the box shut, Billy picked it up and threw the stick to the floor. "That's it," he said, watching the man's face. He wondered if he would be able to get out of the house quickly enough, carrying the heavy box, if the man came after him.

For several minutes, no one spoke. Billy's mother turned finally and pulled at his sleeve, guiding him out of the room. When they reached the living room, she whispered, "Go. Take your jacket and the snakes and go out. Head toward Dr. Corbin's laboratory. Hide there in the brush, where I can find you later, and don't come out until you hear me calling. Please go."

He headed into the cold night air, but went no more than a hundred yards or so and sat down, pulling the box close to him. Bringing his knees up, he gripped them for warmth and sat there, staring back at the house and the pickup truck, still with one door half-open. He wondered what the man would do. Would he burst from the house, trying to find Billy in the predawn shadows? Would he try to catch him and hurt him? Billy wasn't worried about that; he knew the surrounding country far better than the man did, and he could easily lose him among the brush and the dry washes. Still, how long would he have to sit out here? He hadn't really thought about that.

After what seemed a long time—Billy guessed maybe a half hour or so—he saw some slight movement just inside the back door of the house. He jumped up and slipped into a crouch, ready to run if the man came after him.

Finally his stepfather came out, but he was walking slowly, not fast. He stopped and slammed his fist several times against the side of the house. When Billy's mother tried to stop him, he pushed her aside roughly. He began walking forward again. He appeared to stare straight ahead without talking or changing his expression. Billy saw his mother step forward and say something to the man, but he still maintained the same slow, halting pace and did not speak to her.

When he reached the pickup, he stopped, rested his arms on the hood and pressed his face onto his arms, the way a child sometimes does when it cries. Then he shook his head, raised up and walked slowly around the side of the pickup and got in, slamming the door with such force Billy was surprised the window didn't break. He started the engine, jammed the truck into gear and spun out of the yard in a huge cloud of dust with the engine screaming.

Billy didn't move until the sound of the tortured engine had died in the distance. Then he relaxed a little and walked back to where his mother still stood, looking in the direction the truck had gone.

"I don't think he will come back," she said in a low, detached voice when Billy came closer. She didn't turn or look at him, but instead continued to gaze into the distance. "I told him he should stay and forget about the snakes, but something broke inside him. He wouldn't speak to me, and there was no color in his face." She hesitated a moment. "There is something else, too."

"What's that?"

She turned to face Billy. "For some men, strength is everything. They can't stand to be weak. Maybe your snakes scared him so badly he lost something forever. He showed us his fear, and maybe he couldn't stand to look at either one of us again."

"How do you know he isn't coming back?" Billy asked.

"I know. Some things you just feel."

"He hurt you a lot," Billy said, kicking at the dust near his feet. "How do you know he wouldn't hurt you worse the next time?"

"He's gone. I don't think there will be a next time," she said. Then she reached out and put her arm around Billy. Together they stood for several minutes, seeing the first needles of sunlight begin to poke above the far edge of the earth.

She squeezed him more tightly. "We will survive," she said. "We'll probably have to move into Tucson, so I can find work."

Billy hugged his mother. "I'll be right back," he said. He left her there, still gazing at the rising sun, and walked back to where the box was.

He carried the box several hundred yards away, to a series of dry washes dotted with dense thickets of creosote brush and mesquite. "A favor for a favor," he said softly. Holding the box carefully away from him, he flipped the latch and dumped its contents onto the cool ground.

The three diamondbacks and two Mojave rattlers appeared to take a few moments to get used to their surroundings, then each scurried off in the growing daylight. Billy retrieved the box, hoisted it to his shoulder and turned again toward the house. As he walked he began to smile. And soon he began to whistle softly.

The Diving Bear

In the kitchen, Karen's mother gasped and cried out; then Karen heard the storage closet being jerked open and the foosh! thwomp! of the broom as it struck the floor once and then again. "Karen!" her mother called, her voice high-pitched and ragged. "Karen! Get in here *now!*"

Karen leaped from the living-room sofa, where she had been working on a charcoal drawing of old Baxter, the family's beagle, sound asleep on the floor near her feet. Tossing the sketch tablet aside, she almost stepped on one of Baxter's paws as she jumped over him and sprinted through the dining room. Behind her, Baxter suddenly awakened and jumped to his feet, bewildered.

"What's wrong?" Karen cried out, her heart already racing. Reaching the kitchen doorway, she stopped short, hesitated a moment and then cried out, "Mother! Don't kill Tommy!"

In the kitchen, her mother was poised with her broom-weapon high in the air, ready to strike again, while her eyes attempted to follow the rapid, zigzag path of a high-speed fur ball racing back and forth across the kitchen floor.

"I warned you before about that mouse," her mother said, not taking her eyes off the tiny, scrambling form for even a second. "No mice in this kitchen!"

Karen got down on her hands and knees and tried to scoop up her fuzzy friend. At first she missed, but on the second try she got hold of Tommy and picked him up, holding him close to her cheek and talking softly to try to calm him down. "He's a *pet*, Mom," she said, still talking softly. "He's not just some mouse. He's a pet. How could you even think of hurting Tommy?" As she talked, Tommy's tiny nose, like a quivering speck of pink bubble gum, began to poke around and through her fingers.

"Pet or no pet, he doesn't belong in this kitchen." Karen's mother exhaled and slowly lowered the broom. "He nearly gave me a heart attack."

"Maybe I forgot and left his cage unlatched," Karen said. "All he wants to do is look around."

Her mother was still puffing. "He can look around someplace other than this kitchen. You and your animals. I swear, you should live in a zoo."

I'd love to work in a zoo someday, Karen thought a few minutes later as she placed Tommy back in his cage on the desk in her room. Maybe I can be a veterinarian and work with animals all the time.

She rechecked the latch on Tommy's cage, then

checked the latch on a nearby cage in which Marvin, her pet gerbil, was racing happily on a spinning treadmill.

When she returned to the kitchen, Baxter, his tail wagging, padded in from the living room and brushed past her, waiting for her to scratch him behind the ears the way she always did.

She sat down at the kitchen table and idly began to run her hand across Baxter's head. As she did so, her eyes fell on a half-page advertisement in the folded newspaper on the table. "The last, best authentic traveling circus," the ad said. "Lions, elephants, acrobats, clowns, and much more. Fun for the whole family. Come to the Oakwood Mall parking lot and see the raising of the big-top tent on Saturday at 10:00 A.M. Free coupons good for prizes, peanuts, and cotton candy to the first 100 families." The ad had a large, snarling tiger in the center, and in one corner was a drawing of a lion jumping through a flaming hoop.

"Wow! Did you see this, Mom?" Karen jumped from the table, grabbing the paper, and thrust it out for her mother to see. "An old-fashioned *circus!* Coming here!"

"I know, dear," her mother said, glancing at the paper. "But going to the circus is costly. When I was your age, we got into the circus for a dollar or two. Now it's a lot more. I'm not sure we should spend the money for all of us to go."

"Can't you talk to Dad, please?" Karen said, still

holding up the paper. "I may never have a chance to see a circus again."

"I'll talk to him."

Karen couldn't wait to tell her best friend, Denise, about the circus. Denise loved animals almost as much as Karen did. "See if your parents will take you," Karen said. "Maybe we all can sit together."

After Karen's mother mentioned the circus to her dad, he looked doubtful. "Well, there aren't too many circuses around anymore," he said finally. "Maybe we should go."

"Oh, thank you!" Karen said, and gave her dad a hug. When she talked to her friend, however, Denise sounded disappointed. "I can't go," she sighed. "My folks are busy all weekend, and I have to clean my room Saturday."

"Saturday's the only time my parents can go," Karen said.

"Anyway, let me know what it was like," Denise said.

Karen and her parents arrived early at the shopping center. In the parking lot, they saw lean, sun-browned men straining at the ropes and canvas and maneuvering trucks, trailers, and other vehicles into place. They watched as elephants pulled on thick ropes and cables, which in turn lifted the huge big-top tent to its full height.

There was plenty of time before the show, so they

walked around and looked at all the colorful concession stands and displays. The air was full of the thick, musky smells of straw, cotton candy, hot dogs, animals, people, perspiration, and other scents. For the next couple of days, the shopping center parking lot would no longer be just a huge, block-long asphalt slab with places to park cars. In a few short hours, it had been turned into a busy, exciting village filled with performers, exotic beasts, and crowds of eager visitors.

"Let's go behind the big top where the cages are and see some of the animals," Karen said, tugging at her dad's hand.

Her mother hesitated. "I'm not sure people are supposed to go back there."

"Well, one quick look," her dad said, smiling.

Strolling among the cages, Karen and her parents passed a small wooden trailer with a single, barred window. As they passed, they heard a muffled, rumbling sound inside. The trailer shuddered and shook. Leaning closer to look inside, Karen found herself face-to-face with the deep, dark, curious eyes of a large bear. His fur, so dark brown it was almost black, glistened in the tiny patch of sunlight through the bars.

"Mom and Dad! Look here!" she whispered, still staring into the silent, unmoving face.

"You must be interesting-looking," Karen's dad joked softly. "He still hasn't even blinked."

"We're going to get a cup of coffee," her mother said. "You meet us back by the hot-dog stand."

As her parents moved away, Karen lingered a moment. "I'll bet you'd rather run free, wouldn't you?" she said quietly, still staring into the bear's dark eyes. "Too bad you have to be cooped up in that dumb old trailer."

" 'Course he'd like to be free," said a nearby voice, startling her. "All animals would. But we need ol' Blackie here. He's one of the stars of our show." The speaker was a tall, skinny-looking man wearing work clothes and a beat-up old baseball cap. He had a whiskery chin and a toothpick in one corner of his mouth. "Now you know you ain't supposed to be back here, don't you?"

"Well, uh . . ." Karen stammered. "I just wanted a quick peek . . ."

The man smiled at Karen, then scowled and stepped close to the trailer. "Hey! Back in there!" he snarled, giving it a hard slap. Picking up a large piece of wood, he slammed it hard against the bars in the tiny window. When he did, the bear turned away and disappeared into the shadows.

"You come to the big top this afternoon," the man said, turning once again to Karen, "and we'll show you the world's only high-diving bear."

"High-diving?" Karen said, staring first at the man and then back at the barred window in the trailer.

"That's right," said the man. "Ol' Blackie here goes

up on that hydraulic lift over there, and when it's time, he jumps more'n thirty feet through the air into a tank of water."

Nearby Karen saw the mechanical lift platform with a little cage all around it, sitting on a broad, telescoping center support. The whole thing was attached to a tractorlike machine with big rubber tires.

"What if he doesn't want to jump?" Karen asked, turning again to the trailer.

"Oh, the tractor man he just hits a button and that makes a little catch snap open on the platform so it tips, and Blackie takes a dive anyway," the man said. "Ain't no dumb animal gonna mess up the show. But usually we don't have to do that. Blackie's a real show-off. He don't mind at all."

I'll *bet* he doesn't, Karen thought to herself. What kind of animal would ever *want* to fall through the air into a tank of cold water?

"Do you ever think about letting him go?" she asked, glancing from the bear to the man and back to the bear.

"You gotta be jokin', kid." The man smiled broadly and shifted the toothpick from one side of his mouth to the other. "Blackie here's a featured performer. He brings in the crowds. He's a money-maker. We gonna keep this guy around for a long time. Now you run along. Like I said, nobody's supposed to be back here."

As she hurried out of the animal area, Karen

stopped a moment and looked back in the direction of the bear's cage. The skinny man had a large pole which he was poking through a hole in one side of the bear's cage. The man was scowling and yelling something as he did so. Karen felt so sorry for the bear she almost cried.

Karen's mom and dad were waiting by the hot-dog stand. Each was carrying a paper cup filled with coffee. "We'll get you a soda if you like," her mother said. "Then we'd better get in line for our tickets. We'll try to get seats near the center ring."

By show time Karen felt stuffed with hot dogs, cotton candy, peanuts, and soda.

"Takes me back to when I was a kid," her dad said as an acrobatic team made last-minute adjustments on their equipment. The big tent carried the scent of wood shavings, spread over the hard, asphalt surface of the parking lot.

As they watched and waited, scratchy recorded music began to tinkle out through loudspeakers at each end of the tent.

"Oh, look!" her mom said, pointing. "Here come the clowns." They watched as a team of bulb-nosed characters entered the arena in the back of an ancient truck. Her parents chuckled as the clowns jumped out, then began attacking each other with fake baseball bats and firehoses.

In spite of the clowns' antics, however, all Karen could think about was the sad face on the magnificent brown bear.

"Ladies and gentlemen," the announcer finally said, after they had watched trapeze artists, jugglers, jumping tigers, parading elephants, horseback riders, and other acts, "today, as a special treat, we're proud to present Blackie, the world's only high-diving bear."

From a far corner of the big-top tent came the tractorlike machine with the hydraulic arm and the little cage on top. In the cage was the bear, wearing a silly little red hat. He weaved slowly from side to side as the machine moved into the tent toward the center ring. The man Karen had talked to earlier was driving the machine. From another corner came a tractor pulling a wide, flat trailer. On the trailer was a large wooden tank. Water in the tank sloshed over the sides as the trailer rolled toward the center ring.

People around Karen talked excitedly, and several pointed at the bear as the young man guided the machine and the hydraulic platform into position.

"Our friend Blackie used to be an Olympic high-diver," the announcer joked. "Now he just enjoys making a splash for all you folks. Let's give Blackie a big round of applause."

The audience cheered, and many of the children pointed again at the bear in the tiny cage as the machine's arm began to extend and the bear rose into the air.

"Isn't it amazing?" Karen's mom said. "Look how far they can extend that platform thing. And that bear doesn't look too lightweight, either."

It *did* seem amazing that the mechanical arm holding the platform could rise so far. As it extended, the machine's engine sputtered and roared. The bear continued to rise, and as he rose, he shifted from one side to another and back again in his confined space.

Within moments the cage stopped. On the ground, the tractor slowly continued to move the trailer and the large tank until it was in position below the bear. When it stopped, two men stepped to the side of the tank. One, an assistant, was dressed in workmen's clothes. The other, the bear's trainer, wore a sparkling suit and matching top hat with flashy little beads all over.

First, the trainer and his assistant looked up at the cage high above them, then they looked at the tank, to be certain it was in the right position. They yelled something at the tractor driver and he pulled the trailer and tank ahead a foot or so. Then they looked up again, lining up the cage and the tank. Finally they nodded and waved at the driver.

"May we have a drumroll, please?" the announcer said into his microphone. From the loudspeakers came the sound of a drum, first soft and then louder. All eyes were on the small cage high in the air, where the bear continued to shift back and forth and from side to side.

The skinny man Karen had talked to earlier pushed a button on the hydraulic lift and a mechanical arm pulled the front panel of the cage up and out of the way. Karen knew that the man could push another button, too, if he wanted, to send the bear plunging toward the water.

He didn't have to.

The trainer, staring intently at the cage above him, yelled a short, sharp command. After hesitating a moment, the bear edged to the front of the cage, then leaped through the air toward the tank. People in the audience gasped and cheered to see the large animal plunging through the air.

The bear struck the water with a tremendous splash that sent water flying out over the floor of the arena. As the trainer bowed to the cheers of the audience, several assistants quickly boosted a heavy wooden frame with steps over the side of the tank, and the skinny man brought the mechanical arm and cage down to the spot where the steps and tank were attached.

Turning to the tank, the trainer barked several loud commands and the bear slowly climbed up the steps and back into the small cage. The force of the splash had knocked the little red hat off the bear's head, and it now bobbed like a large cork on the water.

"Amazing," Karen's dad said as the hydraulic lift, still holding the caged bear, left the tent.

"I think it's terrible," Karen said. "That can't be very much fun to hit the water that hard. It must be scary, and I'll bet the water's cold, too."

"Well, he doesn't have to hunt for food and he has a place to live," Karen's mother said.

"Hardly living," said Karen, scowling. "All he has

to live in is a crummy little cage. Can we leave? I don't feel like watching any more of this.''

''Oh, don't get so upset,'' said her dad, smiling. ''See over there? Let's watch the high-wire act.''

Karen tried to get interested in watching the wirewalkers, but her thoughts kept returning to the bear, locked in his tiny cage.

All the way home, all she could think of was the bear and what a miserable life he must have. It was pretty obvious the skinny man didn't have any respect for the animal, or he wouldn't treat him the way he did. The more she thought about it, the angrier she became.

Settling into her bed that night, Karen tried desperately to think of other things, as she had before. This time, it was more difficult. In fact, it was downright impossible.

Drifting off, Karen found herself back in the big top among the sights, sounds, and smells of the circus. In front of her, clowns faded and became wirewalkers, and they in turn became animal trainers and trapeze artists. Elephants turned into horses, which became clowns, and they turned into tigers and performing dogs. Impressions and noises swirled together in a carousel of colors and echoes.

She saw the bear again, rising sadly in his tiny cage toward the top of the main tent. Below him, as he rose, the skinny man and the flashy trainer and his assistant were laughing and slapping each other on the back and pointing at the bear. Soon, members of the audience began to laugh and point, too, until the entire big top roared with the clucks and chuckles and guffaws of a thousand chortling voices.

At the center of it all, the bear moved his silent gaze from side to side, trying to shift his great weight within his wretched iron box.

"No! Stop it!" Karen cried out from the audience. "Why are you all laughing? What is the matter with you?"

"Karen? Are you all right?" It was her mother, calling from down the hall. The whirling noise of Karen's dream faded, leaving only the soft silence of her dark room. The clock by her bed showed 3:00 A.M.

"Yeah. Just a dream," Karen mumbled. "I'm okay."

"Some nightmare you had last night," her dad said at breakfast the next morning. "Heard you mumbling and yelling in the middle of the night."

"Dreaming about the circus," Karen said, feeling a little foolish. "Dad, do you think I could go back this afternoon? I could use some of my baby-sitting money. Maybe Denise could come, too. All you'd have to do is give us a ride."

"Are you sure you want to?" He stared at her over his morning paper. "You've *seen* all there is to see."

"Please, Dad? We'll be perfectly safe, and that way Denise can see it, too."

"Well . . ."

"Please, Dad?"

When Karen called her, Denise was excited. "Love to," she said. "I've got baby-sitting money, too. I can't wait."

"I'll be back for you later this afternoon," Karen's dad said as they scrambled from the car near the circus entrance. "Make sure you call me when you're ready to come home."

"This is great!" Denise said, smiling, as they joined the crowd of people moving through the entrance gate. "I haven't been to a real circus since I was a little kid. What do you want to do first?"

"Up to you," Karen said, glancing around. "We could pick up our tickets to the big-top show, and then we could just look around or something until show time."

"Yeah!" Denise said. "Let's start with some real cotton candy."

The crowd was even larger than the day before. Everywhere they went, it seemed, there were more moms, dads, and kids buying snacks, looking at animals, playing concession games and trying to win prizes.

"I gotta get a hot dog," Denise said as they moved through the milling crowd. "And some peanuts, too. Maybe one of those big, warm pretzels. What good's a circus if you don't chow down a little?"

"Tell you what," Karen said, glancing about. "I'm going to get a drink of water. Why don't you find the pretzel stand and the peanut vendor and meet me near the hot-dog stand? Maybe I'll have one, too."

As soon as Denise left, Karen hurried around to the trailers where the animals were kept. She didn't see the skinny man with the whiskery face. In the shadows a few feet away sat the hydraulic machine with its little cage on top. She stared at the machine. It made her mad all over again. It was easy to imagine the great brown bear running free through dense stands of pine and juniper, or sunning himself in the light of a warm spring day, or drinking deeply from some clear, rolling stream. It was far more difficult to imagine him spending his whole life in a tiny box in a world he didn't understand, controlled by people whose only interest was money.

Glancing first one way and then the other, she stepped to the hydraulic machine to look more closely at the way it was all put together. The release catch was no more than a loose steel rod on a rusted spring. It was hooked with a wire to an electrical switch that was connected to a button near the driver. The whole thing looked pretty flimsy.

As Karen started to reach for the steel rod to see how loose it was, someone yelled, "Hey!" behind her.

She jumped, jerked her hand back and spun around.

This time, the skinny man's voice had a hard edge.

"I kicked you out yesterday, and I meant it. Get away from here, or I'll have you thrown out of the circus. And keep your hands to yourself. Nobody touches the equipment but me." As he spoke, he tapped the steel rod with a grimy finger.

Fighting to hold back tears, Karen ran in the direction of the hot-dog stand.

"I gotta quit eating junk," Denise said, holding her stomach and making a terrible face. "If I did this every day, I'd weigh about nine hundred pounds." Hesitating a moment, she looked closer at Karen. "What's wrong?"

"I still feel sorry for the bear," Karen said as they found their seats. "They make him jump into a tank of water. You'll see. And the trainer's assistant is a real jerk."

This time, a capacity crowd filled the big tent as the show began. The same truckload of raucous clowns entered as before, throwing confetti at the people as they passed.

"You okay?" Denise asked, staring at her friend. "You seem like your mind is a million miles away."

"I was just wishing the bear could have a better life," Karen said. "But it's silly to wish. I'll try to forget about it and just concentrate on having a good time."

It was fun seeing Denise enjoying the circus. Karen made an effort to laugh and cheer as the clowns, high-wire and trapeze artists, wild animal trainers, and others performed for the eager crowd.

Finally, the man in the center ring made the same announcement about Blackie, and from the far corner the hydraulic machine with the little cage on top entered as it had the day before. As the machine reached the center ring and the mechanical arm and cage began to rise in the air, the tractor with the flat trailer and the tank of water entered the tent from the opposite corner and began to move slowly toward the center ring.

"He looks nervous," Denise said, staring at the bear in the tiny cage.

He did seem more agitated, Karen thought, watching as the bear rocked from side to side and the great hydraulic arm continued to extend higher and higher. Finally the tiny cage was as high as the hydraulic arm could reach. Once again the machine sputtered and popped but kept running. The skinny man was in the driver's seat, watching the crowd and chewing, as always, on a toothpick.

"I wonder how they're going to get him to jump," Denise said. Her eyes were riveted on the tiny cage, still rocking from side to side. The tractor with the flat trailer and water tank were now approaching the center ring.

Again, as before, the trainer and his assistant measured and checked the bear's position several times. The trainer began guiding the tractor and tank into position. As the tiny cage, high in the air, continued to rock from side to side, the skinny man looked up and scowled. A moment later, clearly irritated, he jumped off the seat of the machine, peered up at the cage and banged his hand on the hydraulic arm several times.

"Looks like he's trying to get the bear to quit moving around," Denise said.

The skinny man turned and began to say something to the other assistant. Suddenly there was a bump and shudder on the long hydraulic arm. In an instant, the crowd screamed as the floor of the tiny cage flopped down, sending the bear plummeting downward, end over end, toward the arena floor.

For a split second, the skinny man didn't appear to understand why the crowd had screamed. Then he looked up again and his eyes widened in terror. He turned and tried to dive out of the way just as the bear slammed to the hard ground, pinning the man's legs.

The stunned driver of the tractor pulling the trailer and water tank slammed on his brakes and stared in shock as the crowd continued to scream. Another assistant ran to the skinny young man, then turned, with the trainer, to the unmoving bear, still enveloped in a small, fluttering cloud of wood shavings. The young man screamed in pain as other circus employees ran to help the trainer yank and strain at the body of the bear until they finally rolled it off the man's crushed legs. Shouting for an ambulance, the trainer sent one of his assistants running out of the tent.

"This is terrible!" Denise cried, her voice barely audible above the screams of people nearby. Her face was shiny with tears. "What on earth happened?"

"Ladies and gentlemen, please remain calm," the announcer said through the loudspeaker, over and over. "This has been a terrible accident. Please remain seated and don't block exits until the ambulance arrives. Please remain seated . . ."

Even after the ambulance people had come and taken the skinny man away, Karen still couldn't make a sound. Moving toward the exit, tears wet on her cheeks, she looked back at the arena floor where the bear lay.

"That skinny guy must have knocked something loose," Denise said. "That's just the worst thing I've ever seen."

Karen nodded, crying softly.

Outside, the stunned crowd moved toward their cars in a distant, roped-off parking area.

"Wait here," Karen managed to say. "I'll call my dad."

She wished she had never ever heard of the circus. It was so horrible, so sad, so terribly *unfair*. She turned one last time to look at the big top. I may never go to a circus again, she thought. If I do, all I'll remember is that beautiful creature, tumbling over and over and over . . .

Standing there, wiping a hand across her cheeks, she was surprised by a sudden, very strange feeling.

The sadness of the bear's death began to dissolve, and in its place came a calm, gentle sense of peace. Now her eyes were playing tricks on her. Where the tent and crowds should have been, a different scene came into clear focus, as though in a dream. A bright mountain clearing opened up, ringed by tall pines. At the center of the clearing was a cheerful little brook, its waves lapping merrily at the rich green tufts of plants and spring-fresh rushes along its sides. And beside the stream stood the bear—looking sleek, strong, and healthy. Sunlight glistened on his fur as he dipped his muzzle to drink from the bubbling, diamond-clear water.

Raising his head again, water droplets running down the fur of his neck, the bear turned and stared at Karen with deep, dark, peaceful eyes. Then the great animal turned and trotted off gracefully, effortlessly toward the tree line, and as he did so the vision faded.

"I'm so glad," Karen whispered, almost afraid to breathe. "Now you're free."

Brothers

From his third-story window overlooking the park, Paul could see most of the ball diamond and even part of the parking lot beyond. By putting his tripod-mounted, 60-power spotting scope on the desktop, he could see close enough to just about tell what color bubble gum the ballplayers were chewing.

Of course, watching from his room as Chris's baseball team practiced was always second-best, regardless of the scope. It didn't matter that he had a big room all to himself with his own computer, his own television set, his own phone, and his own library of video games. It didn't matter that his room was in a large, beautiful stone house that lots of his friends referred to as a "mansion."

He would have given it all up just to be out there with Chris and the other players, all trying to be good enough to make high school varsity some day. Chris was almost two years younger than he, and in many ways he was everything that Paul was not. Barely twelve, Chris already was a strong athlete with a sharp eye and quick reflexes. He was bigger than average for his age, too, while Paul was a little smaller than average for *his* age. The result was that the two boys were nearly the same size, despite the age difference.

Besides being a good second baseman and a decent hitter, Chris also was pretty good at swimming, track, and basketball. He'd probably be a varsity star in not too many years.

He was lucky, too. Just last year, when Chris and their foster father, Don, had taken the family's cabin cruiser out on a Sunday afternoon—just the two of them, "to get to know each other better," Don had said—an explosion on board had trapped Chris below the waterline. He'd managed to kick open a hole and swim to safety—something he might not have been able to do if he hadn't been such a strong athlete.

Paul knew it was useless right now for him even to dream about playing baseball or swimming like Chris did. Although most people were born with normal, healthy hearts, his had some kind of valve that was kind of messed up, doctors had told him, and the muscle was getting weaker, little by little, rather than stronger. A "factory defect" is what he called it when kids asked.

It meant he got tired more easily than Chris and the other kids did. It also meant quite a few visits to Dr. Koenig, their foster parents' heart-specialist friend, and it meant he couldn't do a lot of the things Chris did—like play baseball.

Not that he resented Chris's good fortune. It didn't matter that the two boys weren't really related at all and they were both foster children. Chris was about as good a "brother" as anybody could have. Sure, he was a pain in the butt once in a while, and absent-minded and sloppy about putting away his clothes and not much of a hot shot with his school studies. But he was still a cool kid when you came right down to it. Of course, Paul knew he'd never tell *Chris* that.

Although the boys had separate rooms in the large, rambling house, Chris spent a lot of his time at home in Paul's room. Sometimes it was because Chris needed help with his math or biology or English, and Paul was just the kind of super student who could help. Also, Chris didn't have a television set and video library like Paul's, so he often came to Paul's room to play video games. Other times, they just sat and talked about almost everything. Each felt more comfortable talking with the other than with anyone else in the world.

Several months before, Chris had come into the room one day after basketball practice and flopped, as usual, into the older boy's beanbag chair. "Let me ask you something, Paul," he'd said. "Don't get me wrong. I'm not jealous or nothin', but how come Don and Jeanette keep giving you things like the scope and the TV and stuff, instead of giving us both some things once in a while?" Neither Chris nor Paul referred to their foster parents as "Dad" or "Mom." They'd both tried it for a while, after coming to live in the house, but everyone had soon agreed that it just didn't sound right.

Paul had paused and looked out the window for a while before speaking. "I guess it's because I'm sick. You know, the heart thing. I guess they figure they're helping to balance things out a little. You're an athlete and you're healthy. I'm not saying that's right, but I'm guessing that's why they do it."

"You get good grades, too," Chris said, without anger. "Seems like they're *always* raggin' on me about grades, or this isn't good enough or I forgot to do that. Jeanette especially. I think she hates my guts."

"Naw. They just get strung out. Don comes home from the hospital and he's been in surgery all day and he's tired, and even though Jeanette's at home, they still got a lot of pressure. That's all."

"I don't think it's your heart. I think it's because they know you want to do what *Don* is doing when you grow up—go to medical school and become a big-time doctor and stuff like that. In a way you could almost be like their real son. That kinda thing."

And then Chris had said, as he said nearly every time they talked, "I wish I had a mom and dad."

Paul remembered that conversation now, as he watched Chris and his teammates through the scope. They'd finished practice and Chris already was trotting back toward the house. It was funny watching him swat imaginary pitches and field imaginary grounders as he ran. I wish I still had a mom and dad, too, Paul thought to himself. It had been more than two years since the police officer had come to his house in Santa Cruz and told him and the neighbor lady staying with him for the weekend about the multicar pileup on an ice-slicked highway near Lake Tahoe. In all the pain and confusion and grief, he'd wondered who'd be willing to take care of a kid with heart problems. And fourteen was too young to make it on his own.

Finally, after living for several months with his only other relative—his dad's older sister, Helen—the authorities had lined him up with Don and Jeanette. Their professional backgrounds and willingness to take in foster children had made them seem the perfect candidates.

"You're welcome to stay here with me," Helen had said. "But maybe it's better to have a man's influence in your life, too. Maybe for now the foster home is a good idea."

Chris had come here by another route. Abandoned as a baby, he'd already spent time in five foster homes before being taken in by Don and Jeanette.

How Paul hated sitting here, or sitting on the sidelines at the playing field, watching Chris and the others run and bat and throw. What a fantastic thing it would be to have a strong, healthy heart.

His daydream was shattered by the shrill sound of Jeanette's voice downstairs. "Never!" she screamed. The sound of Chris's voice, lower and more muffled, drifted up, then Jeanette's again. "You know better than that. You come into this house with muddy cleats, muddy pants . . . We are not pigs! Now *get out of here!*"

In minutes Chris, dressed only in his underwear and carrying a clump of muddy clothes, trudged past Paul's room.

Paul pushed his door open farther. "What the heck was that all about?" he asked.

"She's ready to kill me 'cause I got some mud on the floor downstairs," Chris said. He didn't seem overly upset.

"Is she still mad?"

"I dunno. Probably not. She just blows off and then she gets over it. I wish she was more cool, like Don. She talks about having high blood pressure. It's no wonder."

"No kidding."

"Transplants," Don said that evening as the four of them sat at the dinner table. He was a large man with a bushy beard, tangled graying hair, and sharp, penetrating eyes. He always said things in a manner that sounded like he meant business—the same way, Paul imagined, that he probably talked to his patients. "Transplants are pretty common these days and I think we ought to think along those lines for you, Paul. It's not so far-out as it might seem."

"*Heart* transplant?" Paul stopped chewing and stared at the man.

"My gosh!" Chris said, turning to stare at Paul. "That's when they take out somebody else's heart after they get killed or something, and they stick it in your chest, and . . ."

"Chris, please," Jeanette said, scowling at him before turning back to Don. She was a small, nervous woman, a former nurse who was much younger than her husband. She had sharp, almost hawklike features and always seemed to be under one kind of pressure or another. Paul and Chris sometimes joked secretly about the way she always turned red when she got angry—which was nearly every day—and how she sometimes looked like she was about to explode.

"You know what Dr. Koenig has told you," Don said. "A transplant probably is the only choice you'll have, sooner or later."

"Would it make me healthy?" Paul said. He felt curiously nervous just talking about it.

"Dr. Koenig says you could lead a pretty normal life," Jeanette said. "He's the expert."

"But why would you do that for me? You're . . . not even my parents." Paul glanced at Chris, then back at his plate.

"That's another thing we haven't really talked about," Don said, pushing his chair back from the table. "I know the foster-home arrangement means we'd normally keep you for a while, and then you could go on to somewhere else, perhaps to be adopted by an appropriate couple. But since we have no children of our own, Jeanette and I have been considering the possibility of legally adopting you both. We could provide a good home for you. If you're willing, that is."

Both boys said nothing for a moment, shocked into silence by what Don was saying.

"You're talking about us being here for good? Permanently?" Paul finally managed to say.

"Permanently," Jeanette said, smiling at Paul.

"Oh, my gosh," Chris said, smiling slowly as he looked at Paul. The thought of it was mind-boggling. A real family. The thought of it was so exciting he had trouble finishing the rest of his meal. Mostly, he couldn't wait to talk to Paul in his room, away from Don and Jeanette.

"Well, what do you think?" he said, smiling broadly as he plopped into Paul's beanbag chair.

"Kind of a shock," Paul said. "To tell you the truth, I really don't know *what* to think." He liked the idea of a permanent full-time family. On the other hand, he'd *had* a dad and mom whom he remembered very clearly. All this on top of the heart transplant stuff Don was talking about was almost too much to take in one gulp.

"I think it's great," Chris said, still smiling. "Except I still don't think Jeanette's too crazy about me, the way she snaps all the time. Why the heck would she want me around *permanently?* Probably so *you* got somebody to talk to."

"That doesn't make sense," Paul said, scowling. "I think you got it wrong with those two. If they disliked you, they wouldn't be talking about adoption." He smiled. "So, bro, maybe you and me'll each get ourselves a brother out of this."

Chris jumped out of the chair. "Let me use your phone," he said. "I gotta tell Joe and some of the other guys on the team about this."

In spite of everything, Paul couldn't rid himself of a few lingering doubts about the whole arrangement. He decided to go and talk to Don about it. He knew Don would be in his first-floor study, a quiet, book-lined retreat where the man spent many of his evenings after dinner, just unwinding, sorting mail and leafing through medical journals.

"It's not that we in any way want to take the place of your father and mother," Don said, settling back in his chair and staring at Paul. "No one could do that. But you're a fine boy, and this would give you a great future."

"Chris, too," Paul said.

"Of course, Chris," Don agreed. "He's a great kid, too. Together, the four of us could be a real family, don't you think?"

Maybe so, Paul thought as he walked slowly back to his room. Maybe so.

And then there was the transplant idea to think about. Even if it happened, he knew it would be a long time yet. People who are going to get heart transplants, he knew, had to be put on waiting lists, and sometimes it was months and months before they got their new hearts. It was kind of scary. Maybe he didn't want to get on the list. Surgery wasn't exactly something he looked forward to.

"What happens in a transplant?" he asked Don several days later.

"Well," Don said, "I'm not a transplant surgeon, but I can tell you pretty much what's involved. Basically, you have somebody on the waiting list who needs, say, a new heart or a new liver or whatever. They check with the hospital regularly and let the hospital know where they are all the time, in case something comes up."

"Then if somebody else dies . . ." Paul began.

"Well, more or less," Don said. "Sometimes, unfortunately, people die or are killed in car accidents and so forth. When that happens, sometimes their relatives permit their organs, such as the heart or liver, to be put into other people who need them. That way, even in death, they give the wonderful gift of life to other people."

"Pretty nice," Paul said. He'd never thought of it that way.

"It's wonderful," Don said. "There is no greater gift."

"So I'd get on that list, and then wait," Paul said.

"Right. Dr. Koenig already has a lot of information on you—things like height, weight, age, and lots of other facts and test results. That's all on file for the hospital to consider in case a donor organ becomes available. You think about it. There's certainly no rush."

He returned to his room, spun his scope around toward the window and watched Chris's team as it practiced again in the park. How fantastic it must be to have a healthy heart, he thought. To maybe someday do things like hike or play tennis or even whip a ball from third base to first. It was too much to hope for . . .

"What a witch Jeanette is today," Chris said later as he entered Paul's room and flopped down in the chair. He was still wearing the dirt-smeared T-shirt and ripped jeans he'd worn in baseball practice. "All I did was snap up a couple cookies on my way through the kitchen and she practically took my head off. I'm really not sure I want to be part of this family forever. I'm not kidding. What an incredible witch. Won't even talk to me other than to yell."

"I was thinking about the adoption thing," Paul said. "I think we should do it. How often do you get a chance to get a ready-made brother?" He smiled. "Even a no-good like you is better than nothin'."

"Soon as you get your new heart," Chris said, throwing a pillow at Paul, "I'm gonna kick your butt."

In the next weeks Paul became more and more excited about both the surgery and the idea of a "new" family. It just seemed to have so many possibilities. Vacations together. Someone to be there—always—when they came home from class. Someone to be there when they graduated from high school. Somebody to talk to and share things with.

In fact, he was coming to realize something he'd never thought much about before—especially before his parents' accident: most kids take families for granted. Lots of kids don't realize what a wonderful thing it is to belong somewhere, and to someone. It was something his real parents certainly would have understood.

The better he felt, however, the worse Chris seemed to become. In the following weeks, Paul noticed he didn't laugh as much as he had in the past, and Chris was grumpy far more often than he had been.

"It's Jeanette," Chris said, when Paul asked him again what was wrong. "All I ever hear is 'don't do this,' and 'you can't do that,' and 'get out of there,' and 'knock it off.' What a rotten personality. And Don, too. Even *he* seems to be raggin' on me all the time. I swear, sometimes I think if I was their real kid, I'd run away."

"I still think they don't mean anything," Paul said. "They've been pretty decent to me. Don got me registered for that heart stuff at the hospital, and they're taking me to see Dr. Koenig again. That's probably all on their minds. I really think when we get the adoption and surgery thing out of the way, they'll be different. Maybe they can relax a little then."

"Fat chance," Chris said. "In fact, I was gonna talk to you about the adoption thing. I made up my mind. Jeanette's got such a terrible temper and always yelling and stuff, I just don't want to live here. Even with everything that's here. You know, you and I can be like friends and write letters to each other and all, but I just don't want to live here and have cranky people around, yelling at me 'till I'm grown up. She even threw a hamburger bun at me the other day when I asked where they were."

Paul turned and stared out the window. "I thought maybe we both had a shot at getting a family, *being* a family . . ."

"I don't know," Chris said. "I'm just telling you what I think."

"Well, don't tell them anything." Paul turned to face Chris. "Maybe we can still work something out. Maybe I can talk to them."

"Good luck," Chris said, without smiling.

All that evening Paul thought about what Chris had said. He decided he'd talk to Don when he came home the next day. Just lay it straight on him. Just ask him flat-out why they seemed to be so hard on Chris. If it made Don mad, then it would just have to make him mad. After all, the family thing was a good idea, and Don and Jeanette were risking screwing it all up for good.

"It's interesting you should mention it," Don said after Paul had brought up all the yelling and the way

Chris felt he was picked on. "Jeanette and I have talked about it, too. We're realizing that we've been awfully one-sided in our treatment of you guys. We thought so much about your heart problem and the adoption thing, we forgot to be fair. We thought we'd talk to Chris about it, and reassure him that things are going to change. In fact, we're going to redo his room and make it like yours."

"That's great," Paul said. "That's really great. I'll talk to him, too, and let him know that things are gonna get worked out."

"No, we'd like to surprise him with the room idea," Don said, smiling. "We want to see his face when we tell him. In fact, we'd like to go all out and get him his own computer, his own TV, and everything else."

Later, at dinner, both Don and Jeanette were friendly, and they all laughed when Chris told about a kid on his team who'd gotten in trouble for painting their team name in orange metallic paint on his dog—and on the neighbor's dog, too.

I wonder when they'll spring it on him, thought Paul. Maybe they'll wait until bedtime, or maybe they'll announce it at breakfast tomorrow morning. I'd love to have a camera ready when they tell him he's getting a bigger room and his own TV. I hope he doesn't do something dorky like get mad anyway and tell them it's too late and he's leaving, TV or no TV. Naw. He's smarter than that.

The next day, he couldn't stand it any longer. He *had* to know when Chris was going to be told. Jeanette was gone to one of her club meetings. He decided to wait quietly in Don's office for him to come home from the hospital, so he could ask Don without Chris knowing about it.

He sat for a while in Don's leather chair in the book-lined office, looking at the hundreds of volumes, almost all of them on medical and surgical subjects. Boy, you sure have to learn a lot to be a doctor—any kind of doctor, he thought. I wonder if I'll be able to remember it all if I go into medicine.

Turning in the swivel chair, he gazed out through the window at the park where Chris and three of his friends were tossing a Frisbee around. That's me, guys, he thought, smiling. Just give me a new heart, and I'll be out there with you. Boy, I can't wait.

Swinging around in the chair, he looked absently at the desk clock. Don was due home before long, unless he got hung up somewhere. He fiddled idly with a pen on the desk and moved the center drawer in and out a couple of times. As he absently pulled it out again, a file folder inside the drawer caught his eye. The folder had "Paul" written in pencil on the outside.

He knew he shouldn't be digging around in Don's desk, but now he was curious about the folder. Glancing quickly toward the door, he slid the folder from the drawer and peeked inside. It contained only a single sheet of paper on which were typed several figures under two main headings: "Chris" and "Paul." Under both were subheadings like blood type, age, height, weight, allergies, and other categories.

My gosh, he thought. This is some kind of health report or something. What the heck . . . Then his eyes fell on a single phrase typed at the bottom of the page. It said, "Surgical compatibility—donor/recipient: Excellent."

Donor-recipient. Paul silently formed the words over and over again. Donor meant the "giver." Recipient meant the "receiver." I still don't get it, he thought. And then a sudden thought struck him so hard it nearly took his breath away. He gasped and reread the figures on the typed sheet. No, it couldn't be. They couldn't be considering Chris as a heart *donor* and himself as a heart *recipient*. Chris's heart? If that were true, it meant they were planning to . . .

He could scarcely breathe. He raced to the front door and shouted at Chris, waving him in when he looked in the direction of the house. Chris tossed the Frisbee at one of the other boys and jogged over.

"Yeah? Make it quick, will ya?" Chris said. "We got a throwin' contest going."

"You gotta come in here," Paul said, still gasping.

"You look awful," Chris said. "You sick?"

"Look at this." Paul pushed the folder into Chris's hands.

"What's it mean?" Chris asked, casually scanning the figures.

"I don't know," Paul said. "But it looks kinda like Don and Jeanette were thinking about *you* as a heart donor."

"Me? How the heck could *I* be a donor?"

"I don't know. But there's only one way to be a donor."

Chris hesitated a moment and looked at Paul. *"Wait a minute.* You mean . . ."

"I don't know. What do *you* think this means?"

"This is sick!" Chris said, looking around and then back at the folder. "Maybe I better get the heck out of here."

"I'm calling my Aunt Helen," Paul said, "before Don and Jeanette get back."

Both boys went to Paul's room. Chris stood near the door, watching, while Paul dialed.

"I can't believe anyone's plotting anything as wild and crazy as murder," she said, after Paul had explained about the folder. "I'm sure if you go and talk about it, you'll find there's a perfectly logical explanation. When you've ironed it all out, if you both would like to come up here to Portland for a visit, maybe just to get away for a while, you're more than welcome to stay as long as you wish."

"We gotta talk to Don and Jeanette about this,"

Paul said as soon as he had hung up. "And we gotta do it together. I'm gonna take this folder and hide it in my room."

Both boys paced nervously back and forth in Don's office as they waited for the faint sound of the garage door opening. Finally, when the sound came, they both jumped and Chris's eyes grew wide with alarm. "I can't take this," he said, starting for the door. "I gotta get out of here."

"No! We gotta do this together," Paul hissed. "You *stick around!*"

Don entered the office humming and tossed several papers on the chair in the corner. He smiled when he saw the two boys.

"Can we talk for a minute?" Paul said, straining to sound calm and as normal as possible.

"Sure. Shoot," Don said as he plopped into the chair behind the desk.

"When's Jeanette coming home?" Paul tried to lean casually against the far wall in front of the desk. Chris slid down slowly until he was seated on the carpeted floor with his knees drawn up and his hands resting on his knees.

"Be here in a second." The man leaned back and loosened his tie. "She was right behind me when I turned into the driveway." He stared at both boys and smiled. "Must be something important. You both look so serious."

"Naw," Paul lied. "We just wanted to talk to you

both about something that's important to us. Thought this might be a good time."

Don nodded just as Jeanette looked into the office. "I ordered a pizza for the boys for dinner," she said, smiling. "Remember, you and I have to be at the Channings' for dinner at eight."

"The boys are right here," Don said. "Come on in for a minute. Something they want to talk to both of us about."

She stepped into the office and nodded at Paul and Chris. "Gotta hurry," she said. "I need to get dressed for dinner."

Paul's heart was beating fast—too fast—and he could feel that his face was flushed. He glanced and saw that Chris was staring rigidly at the floor.

"Remember the heart transplant thing?" Paul said, afraid his voice might show how nervous he was.

"Of course." Don picked up a pencil and began to doodle on the desk pad.

"Who did you figure would be the donor?"

There was a silence in the room as Paul glanced at Don, then down at Chris, who still was staring rigidly at the floor. Don, in turn, glanced at Jeanette and then back at Paul.

He cleared his throat. "Well," he said calmly, "as I explained to you, it's necessary to wait until a suitable donor becomes available. Remember how we talked about that? Sometimes people are in accidents, or they die for whatever reason, and if certain things match, then a heart or liver can be taken out of them and put into someone who needs it."

"So you said I'd be on a list, and then wait until that happened."

"Sure. Why?"

Paul cleared his throat. His heart was still beating fast, and he was beginning to feel a little faint.

"I found the folder in your desk. The one where you have me and Chris as 'recipient' and 'donor.' "

There was another long silence in the room. Glancing at Jeanette, Paul saw that her face was beginning to turn dark red.

Don's voice remained even. "Paul," he said, "first of all, why were you poking around in my desk? Second, that folder doesn't mean what you think it does. I was simply thinking of body types and so forth, trying to think of things that would help you. You absolutely got the wrong impression with that folder. Good grief! You thought Jeanette and I . . ." His voice trailed off. Paul noticed that his face was beginning to turn red, too.

"I've already told my Aunt Helen in Portland about it," Paul said, his voice wavering, "and I hid the folder. I forgot to remind her, but I will, about the boat explosion last year, too. Just you and Chris alone on the boat, Don. Remember?"

Jeanette's voice was a strangled gasp. "You called your aunt and told her *what?*"

"I told her I thought you two were planning on

doing away with Chris, somehow, so I could get his heart. I'm gonna show the folder to the police, too."

"Why, you incredible little . . ." Jeanette lurched forward, her face twisted in a snarl of pure, unbridled rage. She opened her mouth to speak again, but all that came out was a gagging, gasping sound. She put one hand to the side of her head and her eyes began to roll back in her head. Chris jumped to his feet and stepped back as she sank to her knees and flopped face-forward on the carpet.

"Jeanette!" Don shouted, leaping around the desk and kneeling beside her. He pressed his fingers under the side of her jaw, looked into her eyes for a moment, then jumped to his feet and furiously dialed the telephone. "Emergency!" he barked into the phone, shouting the numbers of the address into the mouthpiece. "Possible serious stroke or cerebral hemorrhage!" He slammed the receiver down and dropped to the floor again beside the still form of Jeanette. "Get out of here!" he shouted to Chris and Paul. "Just get out of here!"

Chris moved slowly, cautiously, up to the side of the bed, taking care not to bump anything or get tangled in all the tubes and equipment. He stood for several seconds without speaking as Paul's eyes slowly opened and his head moved just a little on the pillow. Paul had oxygen lines in his nose and other lines with some kind of liquid going into his arm. All kinds of strange equipment with lighted panels and switches stood near the bed.

A nurse was leaning close to one of the machines, watching the numbers. Paul's Aunt Helen stood near the nurse. "Just a few seconds," she half-whispered. "He has to rest."

Paul looked strange with all the equipment around and all the tubes in him. Chris spoke in a low voice, almost too low to hear, then cleared his throat and spoke again a little louder. "Doctor thought it would be good if we saw each other for a second or two," he said. "You okay?"

Paul nodded slightly. His eyes closed, then opened again.

"We gotta go," Chris said, "but me and Aunt Helen'll be back every day."

"Thank you," Aunt Helen said to the nurse as they walked quietly from the room. Turning to Chris, she said, "Normally they wouldn't let us in this part of the hospital. Especially with this kind of surgery. But Dr. Rizek thought seeing you would be good for Paul and help him recover faster."

"Foggy," Chris said, turning to look outside as they passed a window in the corridor.

Aunt Helen put an arm around his shoulders. "Gets that way a lot this time of year in Portland. You'll get used to it."

"Is Paul going to be okay?" Chris asked.

Aunt Helen smiled. "I think so."

"Isn't it funny," he said, without smiling. "Looks like Jeanette and Don might have been plotting something. Instead, Jeanette dies. Don's trying to get himself out of trouble, so he arranges for Paul to get *her* heart. Weird. At least with Jeanette's heart, maybe now Paul can have a normal life."

"I certainly hope so," said Aunt Helen.

"It's wild," Chris said softly as they reached the elevator. "It's just so wild."

Beyond the Door

Ever see the inside of a watch?

I mean a *real* watch, with teeny little springs and gears and jewels—not just some electronic digital job with nothin' but a computer chip inside? A real watch is fantastic, with all those tiny pieces working together. It just blows my mind the way it all works. I guess I've always enjoyed messing around with gears and levers and you-name-it.

In my family, gadgets and gizmos just seem to be part of the natural surroundings. Somebody's always got this or that thing apart, and somebody's always trying to wire this doodad or repair that thingamajig. That's what my dad calls things that he doesn't have names for. Like he'll say, "Hey, Jack! Gimme that thingamajig over there on the floor." And somehow, you always know what he wants, just by the way he says it.

He loves to fix lawn mowers and cars and darn near everything else that runs or hums. Even when he was little, I guess he was always tearing something apart and putting it back together.

He doesn't do it for a job or anything. During the day he works in an office, just like lots of other people. When he fixes stuff, it's just for fun.

Well, my ma says I inherited a pretty good dose of that, 'cause I get a lot of fun out of doing the same thing. Except I'm not as good as my dad, of course. On the other hand, I *have* taken my bike apart, including the gears for all ten speeds, about a million times. I goofed it up a few times, but heck, it works okay now.

A bike's pretty important in Florida. We're on the Gulf side, not too far from Tarpon Springs. A lot of old guys who live around here used to be sponge divers, making their living going down in the ocean to get the sponges. It's warm here all the time, so you can ride a bike all year long and not worry about things like snow and ice.

My brother, Cameron, and I ride our bikes all over town when we're not playing ball or going to school or helping our dad fix things around the house. Cameron's eleven, which makes him not quite two years younger than me. He's my brother and all, but sometimes he does things that are so dumb you wouldn't believe it.

Like, twice he's lost the key to his bike lock—*after* he'd locked up his bike. And once he managed to get himself caught in our utility shed with the lawn mower after he snapped a combination lock on the *inside* and didn't know the combination. My dad had to make a hole in the door to get at the lock—and at Cameron.

That was about a year ago. After it happened, I sort of got interested in locks and how they work, I guess 'cause they're sort of gadgets, too. I bought a cheap padlock at the hardware store and played around with it, and then I started getting a few books out of the library about locks and all the different kinds that are used. You wouldn't believe how many there are. They got locks of every possible kind, from fancy little things you put on your luggage for show when you travel, all the way up to those incredible heavyweight jobs that are used on bank vaults and things.

I finally told my dad that when I get a few years older, I'd like to take one of those correspondence courses you see advertised all the time that show you how to become an expert on locks. I could get money for grinding keys, too.

I even asked my dad if I could buy a real set of "picks" like the experts use, so I could practice opening different kinds of locks. He said, no way. "In the first place," he said, "if you get something like that, you're going to be tempted to try and open things you shouldn't. In the second place, if the police ever caught you with something like that, they'd probably wonder whose locks you were trying to get into."

Just for fun (when my dad didn't know it) I made a few little pick-like things anyway, out of different kinds of wire. They weren't great but they kind of worked.

The more I studied locks and stuff, and experimented with the little ones I bought, the easier it became to open locks around our house.

Don't get the wrong idea here.

It's not like I started going around spying on people or anything, but I *did* find out that most locks around a house can be opened—even when they're locked—about as easy as opening a can of beans.

But, like I said, I didn't go around spying or anything. Well, only once. Cameron was taking a bath one night with the door locked. He'd been kind of a jerk that day anyway, so I picked open the lock with a heavy piece of wire and I threw a pitcher of ice water into the tub. I got punished, of course. It was worth it.

Other than that, I pretty much stayed with my own locks, as far as the picking went. That is, until I noticed the rusted padlock on the front door of an old abandoned house that sat a few miles outside our town, along a twisty, winding road that wasn't even paved and wasn't used much any more. I saw the house one Saturday when my friend Alan and I were taking a bike hike inland, away from the coast.

Sometimes you see houses like that, where the owners have been gone a long time ago and people have smashed out the windows and there isn't much left except creaking boards and cobwebs and wind. I always wonder what the people were like who lived in a place like that. You know, were they nice people, did they have kids, why did they leave, things like that.

This place had vines and junk all over, and it looked like rot had just about eaten most of the wood clear through. It was easy to imagine snakes all over inside, and maybe even a 'gator or two in the low-lying swamp that started just behind the place. The roof boards were rotted, and the front porch looked like you'd go straight through, even if you were skinny like Cameron and weighed half of nothin'.

The lock on the front door didn't make a bit of sense, considering the condition of the house. Maybe that's why I thought it was kind of interesting. I kept thinking about that lock all the rest of the day, and later I told Alan I'd like to go back and take a look at it.

"Who cares about some dumb ol' lock?" Alan said, after we'd parked our bikes under an old red cedar tree near the road and were eating our sandwiches.

"Well," I said, "you wonder why somebody put it on there. I mean, you could crawl right in through the window."

Alan snapped open a soda. "Somebody probably put it on a long time ago," he said, burping as he said it. "Anyway, let's just head home. You can go check out the lock on your own sometime."

I decided to do exactly that a week or so later, without Alan.

When I rode up on my bike, the place looked the same, which I guess wasn't too surprising. It had a real lonely look, like something lost and forgotten, which it was.

The boards on the front porch creaked like crazy when I stepped on them, and one even broke about halfway through when I put my weight on it. I tried not to make any fast movements. I kept imagining some big, hungry 'gator below the porch, grinning and waiting for dinner to arrive in the form of my leg.

The lock was a standard type, pretty much a larger version of one I had fooled around with at home. It looked rusted all through, but surprisingly it snapped open after I diddled around for a while with my little wire pick. The door was soft and rotted, and I almost expected it to fall into the house when I pushed on the rusted knob.

There was no way I was ready for what I found inside.

I mean, there are some things you can't even tell people without them thinking you're nuttier than a holiday fruitcake.

I figured the boards inside would be as rotten as the porch ones, so I stepped veeerrry lightly inside.

As I did so, the door gently swung closed behind me. That in itself gave me a definite surprise. It was nothing, though, compared with what I saw straight ahead.

The boards inside weren't rotten at all. In fact, they were polished hardwood. From inside, the windows looked unbroken and clean—almost new, in fact. The house was furnished, with braided rugs on the floor, plain cloth curtains on the windows, and heavy furniture that looked handmade. Near one end of what must have been the dining room was a large stone fireplace with a cheerful little blaze going. Several black iron pots were hung on a rod across the fireplace not far from the flame.

Somebody's gotta be kidding, I thought. A *fire* in the fireplace? At this time of year? In *Florida?* But the funny thing is, it wasn't overly warm in the room. In fact, it was slightly chilly. The trees and things I could see through the windows didn't look like red cedar and swampland, either. They looked more like what you'd see up north.

At the center of this room was a large, heavy-looking table. As my eyes adjusted to the light, I realized with a jolt that people were seated at the table. They looked to me like a father, mother, and two children—a girl about my age and a younger boy. They all looked up as I entered. The girl seemed to blush a little and looked back down at her lap. The man, though, nodded at me without speaking, and gestured at me to come all the way into the room.

They all had on the weirdest clothes you ever saw. The guy had on this sort of severe-looking black coat, buttoned way up, strange-looking pants that stopped at the knees, high white socks, and rough-cut shoes, each with a little buckle on the top. He had a short beard, but no moustache. And he had a lousy haircut.

The woman and the girl were dressed pretty much the same. Each had on a very long, plain dress, way high on the neck and long sleeves, too, and each wore a puffy, white cloth kind of cap over her hair. No makeup and no earrings. The boy was dressed sort of like his dad, and he had a bad-looking haircut, too.

They all were eating off what looked like pewter plates. Probably having chicken or goose or something, from the smell of it. Other than from the fire, the only light came from the windows and a pair of drippy, flickering candles in old-fashioned holders on the table.

"Gosh, I didn't know anybody was in here," I said, kind of stumbling in my speech. "I didn't mean to break in, honest."

"Pray thee, come and sup with us," the man said, gesturing again. He didn't smile, but his face seemed mostly kind. In fact, he looked like a real decent guy.

I was really too scared to do much of anything, so I slowly sat down near the little boy. The woman still didn't say anything. She just got up, went over by the fireplace and came back with a drumstick and some vegetables on a pewter or tin kind of plate.

"Man, I feel like a real dork barging in on you like this," I said. "You gotta understand, I'm no housebreaker."

"I am John Wexford, late of Plymouth Colony, and this is my wife, Elizabeth," the man said. "These are our children, William and Hester." When he said this, the girl got all red again and stared at the floor.

The way they sounded, I knew they sure as heck weren't from Florida.

"By what name are you called?" the man said.

"Jack Hillier," I said. "Well, John, but everybody calls me Jack."

"What meaneth this word, 'dork'?" the man asked, still not smiling.

"Well," I said, "it's kinda like 'nerd' or maybe 'jerk.' Somebody who's kinda out of it, I guess."

"Dost thou not pray before thou eatest?" the kid asked softly, when he saw me take a bite out of the drumstick.

"Well, uhh . . . yeah, probably should," I mumbled. "Fact is, I'm not very hungry." I laid the drumstick back on the plate. "Where you people from?" I added, figuring it couldn't hurt to make a little conversation.

"Late of Plymouth Colony," the man said again. "Prior to that, of Tealshire-on-Thames in England, from which we sailed in the year of our Lord, sixteen-hundred and thirty-seven, never to return."

Sixteen-thirty-seven? I thought. This guy is cuckoo. And they gotta be from a strange place. "Never been there," I said. "My dad flew to London on business last summer, though. Said everything was super expensive."

When I said this, the little boy snorted and began to giggle. When his father scowled at him, he looked at the floor and tried to stop, but his shoulders still jumped every so often.

"Wouldst thou kindly explain 'flew?' " the man said. "Surely thy father hath not wings."

"Seven-forty-seven," I said. "Went on United, I think."

"Perhaps our young visitor hath a fever," the lady said softly. Her eyes seemed kind and motherly.

"Thou mayest stay with us till thou regain thy health," the man said, "if it be thy wish."

"No thanks," I said, rising slowly. "I gotta go. Thanks . . . uh . . . for the offer." I moved toward the door, stifling the urge to run like a bandit. As I stepped outside I looked back, and they were all still seated at the table, looking silently in my direction.

I don't absolutely, positively believe this, I thought to myself. Obviously, the pastrami-and-cheese sandwich I ate earlier must have gone real bad in the heat.

Outside, the Florida sun and moist air hit me like a whack in the face. It was easily 85 degrees in the shade. From the yard, the house looked like before, with broken-out windows, sagging walls, and an almost-collapsed roof.

It took me more than two weeks to convince Alan that I wasn't just inventing some stupid joke about the people in the house.

"Only one thing to do," he said. "We gotta go out there. And if you made this up, say good-bye to your soccer ball I borrowed. I'll keep it forever, I swear." He insisted on bringing his dad's expensive camera, too (unknown to his dad), in case we found something to take a picture of.

The next Saturday we filled a bag with sodas, chips, and four candy bars, and we threw in Alan's dad's hunting knife, just to be on the safe side. Cameron didn't know about the people, but he wanted to go riding with us. I promised him he could use my baseball glove for a week if he'd stay home.

The old house looked exactly the same as before. The lock, to my surprise, was closed again, the way I'd first found it. Luckily, I still had a piece of wire in my bike handlebar bag. It took me about five minutes to snap the lock open.

"Okay, you go first," Alan said, fiddling nervously with the hunting knife.

"You go," I said. I felt a little strange about just bolting through the door, the way I had before.

"Forget it," Alan said, turning toward the yard. "I ain't goin' in first, no way, no how."

"Okay, okay," I whispered. "But you follow me close."

Inside, the floor was smooth hardwood, just like

before, and the curtained windows looked clear. "Holy cow . . ." Alan whispered. His eyes were big and his mouth hung open. Again, there was a large stone fireplace, and inside it, a small crackling fire. This time, however, the furniture was different. Some of the furniture looked heavy and homemade, but some of the pieces had little curlicues and fancy things. There was a long, flintlock rifle on the wall over the fireplace, and a powder horn hanging near it on a leather thong. The dining-room table was different, too, with curved, fancy legs on it. And the people were *really* different.

At one end sat a guy in a kind of plain white shirt and heavy wool pants. He had a huge, bushy beard and moustache. At the other end of the table was a woman in a long, bright cotton dress that had a little ruffle around the collar. The woman's hair was drawn back into a big, kind of round bunch in the back, and she had a ribbon in it.

On the far side of the table was a guy you had to see to believe. He was big, with a bushy beard and eyebrows, and he was dressed entirely in fringed buckskins, right down to beaded and fringed buckskin moccasins on his feet. He had huge, rough-looking hands, feathers hanging in a small bunch in the front of his leather "shirt," and a knife in his belt so big it made Alan's dad's blade look like a toothpick.

The man and woman on each end of the table seemed to be eating pretty normally, but the guy in the leather had both arms on the table and was tearing meat off a bone with his hands. The smell of roast hung in the air like a veil.

Just like the guy on my first visit, the guy in the white cloth shirt motioned for us to come in, and again the door closed softly by itself.

"Set and eat!" the guy in buckskin said. He had a thunderous voice, and smacked a lot as he chewed. "You et yet?"

Neither Alan nor I could make a sound, even though we tried.

"Where you boys hail from?" the big man said, dropping the bone onto his plate.

"N-Not far from here," I said, and cleared my throat.

"Y-yeah. Near Tarpon Springs," Alan said. "We've lived here in Florida all our lives."

"*Florida?*" the man said. He threw back his head and laughed so loud both Alan and I jumped. He laughed again, and the other man and woman began to laugh, too. "Why, you ain't in Florida, boy! This here's Saint Louis! I think you boys been in the locoweed." He stopped laughing then, and stared at us for a moment. "You're dressed mighty strange, too, I'd say. You boys tryin' to put one over on us?"

"No, sir," I managed to say.

"Well, I tell you what," the man said, leaning back in his chair and folding his arms. "My sister, Louisa, here, and her husband, Henry, been nursing me back to health ever since I took a Ree arrow in the shoulder last spring. But now I'm fit, and a bunch of us is plannin' to take keelboats up the Missouri to the Yellowstone River country. Due to head out this very afternoon. From the Yellowstone we'll be headin' into the high country to trap beaver over the winter. We could use a couple good hands. Either of you boys up for a little gen-u-ine adventure?"

"Well, I don't . . ." Alan said, his voice trailing off.

"Sure you are," the man said, smiling. "This here's a chance to join the Rocky Mountain Fur Company."

"I wrote a paper about the fur trade," I whispered to Alan. "My gosh, that was in the *eighteen-twenties* . . ."

The man must have had ears like a deer. "It happens to be eighteen and twenty-three," he said, "in case you boys haven't seen a calendar—or can't read one."

"That's it for me," Alan said softly, backing toward the door. "I'm outa here."

"Boys, you're missing a great chance here," the man said, still smiling as both Alan and I stepped out into the thick Florida sunshine.

"You wanna tell me what just happened in there?" Alan said, his eyes wide. He kept moving his head back and forth between me and the house. "And *lookit*. From out here, it looks like the windows are all broken out and the wind is whistling through."

"*Now* will you believe me about the other people?" I said.

"I'll tell you," Alan said, his voice still a half-whisper. "Either I can't wait to come out here again, or I never want to see that place again. I haven't decided which."

The next Saturday, curiosity won. We headed out again with the same kind of supplies and the camera. "This time I'm gonna get some kinda picture," Alan promised.

Although we were prepared for something strange, this trip through the door was the biggest shocker of all.

This time I didn't even recognize the room as a dining room at all. A color video screen covered one wall, and the floor was like a diamond-bright mirror. The furniture was all molded into strange shapes, and people dressed in what looked like foil jumpsuits were eating something they were squeezing out of foil tubes.

The weirdest thing was *nobody spoke*. They looked at us kind of bug-eyed and we understood what they were thinking. Like, they were thinking, "Come and eat with us," and we *understood!* You could see—I couldn't believe it—white drifts and frost outside through the windows, right here in the middle of *Florida!* The windows looked like some kind of special plastic.

"Is that *snow* outside?" Alan whispered to me.

"The earth has shifted," one of the people, a woman, beamed to us without opening her mouth.

"Florida now has an Arctic climate. The change be-gan several hundred years ago, in the late nineteen-nineties . . ."

"My gosh . . ." Alan's voice was half-moan, half-whisper. The camera fell out of his hands onto the floor as he and I bolted for the door. He didn't stop running, with me close behind, until he reached the tree near the road where we'd left the lunch. Both of us stared at each other, too scared out of our minds to make a sound, not certain whether we should tell someone or try and forget everything.

"Darn it!" Alan said suddenly, gazing back at the house. "My dad's camera! I gotta have that camera or my dad'll kill me."

"Forget the camera!" I hissed. "Just stay outa there!"

"I can't," Alan said, moving again toward the house. "I swear, my dad likes that camera more'n he likes his car."

"Forget it!" I yelled. "I'm not movin'."

"Don't," Alan yelled. "But that camera's comin' out or I don't go home."

Now, I admit, I was crazy with fear. I didn't have the foggiest idea what was going on, but it looked to me like there was a good chance I'd never see Alan again. People from the past, people from the future, Florida turnin' into some kind of Arctic place and talkin' about *snow* in the warmest, sunniest place I know of . . .

What a stupid idea it was to fiddle with that old lock, I thought. I swear, I told myself, if he comes out with that camera, I'll never touch a lock again.

Well, a minute or two passed and I'm about going crazy when out ran Alan, faster than I ever saw him run before. He had the camera in one hand and he was waving the other. "I got it!" he yelled. "Let's get the heck out of here!" He must have run half a mile alongside his bike, just hanging on to it, before he even got on. We both set a speed record getting back to my house.

"I think we stumbled onto one of those strange zones you hear about," Alan said, still puffing, as we drank the last of the sodas in my backyard. "Like the Bermuda Triangle or somethin'. One little spot where time doesn't mean anything and everything's screwed up. Can you believe it? Crazy. The camera was still on the floor. Darn good thing. Now my dad won't murder me."

My stomach was still feeling pretty topsy-turvy. "No more locks. I swear. Not anymore. If I live to be three-hundred, I'm never gonna pick another one. I may never even *use* a lock again."

"Unless we want people to think we each got a screw loose, we better never tell anybody about this," Alan said. "And I mean *nobody*."

Right then and there, Alan and I made a pact that we would never go near that old house again. We promised each other faithfully. We swore we'd keep the promise forever.

That lasted about a week. The curiosity was killing both of us.

This time, we packed *two* knives, plus a wire to pick the lock, and Alan left his dad's camera at home. "Nothing to take a picture of, anyway," he said, trying to sound bolder than he was. "I'm sure we just *imagined* all that junk."

When we rounded the final turn on the way to the old house, we were both too nervous to speak. Walking our bikes and trying to make no sound, we were prepared for almost anything—except what we found. Where the house had sat there was nothing more than a small pond. The sides were choked with reeds and dense grass. A couple of moss-covered trees on the far side looked as though they'd been there forever. Birds flitted and chirped among the taller reed stalks.

"That does it," Alan said, matter-of-factly. "Now I know I'm crazy. Check me into the funny farm and throw away the key."

I couldn't believe it. Leaning my bike on the same tree as before, I walked to the edge of the pond. The ground was spongy. Old weeds, sticks, and leaves were scattered and buried, undisturbed, in the marshy soil. It seemed like maybe even a fish or two might be moving about in the pond's clear water.

"Glad you were here," I said finally to Alan. "Nobody would've believed this if I hadn't had a witness."

"Now I *know* it was our imagination," Alan said. "And I'm glad. As long as we know that, we can relax a little."

On a whim, I decided to take off my shoes and socks and wade a short distance into the clear water. It was cool, and felt great after biking in the Florida heat. On the sparkling surface of the pond I could see the reflected sky and clouds. It was hard to believe that anything other than this pond had been here for ten thousand years. In fact, I was about convinced it *had* been here for thousands of years, and the house was just some weird dream that happened to hit Alan and me.

Looking back, I saw that Alan had settled down under the tree and had pulled his cap over his eyes. Grabbing a snooze under a tree on a lazy warm day seemed like a great idea. I decided I'd join him.

I couldn't believe the water was so cool and glassy. On its surface, reflections of even the smallest birds could be seen high overhead. I looked over again at Alan, and when I casually turned my gaze back to the water, my heart darn near stopped. I saw my reflection all right, but also reflected in the water, behind and beside me, were the guy with the bad haircut and the mountain man and a bunch of other strangers. They were sort of leaning forward, where

I could see them in the pond's surface, and they were just staring.

I spun around so fast I sloshed water clear back to the grassy bank. When I did, the people in the water vanished. At the noise, Alan jerked his head up, pulled off his cap and stared at me. There was nothing between Alan and me but the bank, the weeds, and the same grassy strip as before.

"What the heck was *that* all about?" Alan asked, scowling.

"Guess I lost my balance," I stammered. "Let's go get an ice cream."

As we walked away with our bikes I decided I wouldn't tell Alan and shake him up. At least not right now. And I wasn't about to look back. Who knows what might have been standing by the pond, watching us?

"You know," Alan said, after we'd walked for a mile or so, "I still wonder why we imagined we saw those people in the house before."

"Me too," I said, keeping my eyes straight ahead. "I guess some things in life you're better off just not knowing."

The Substitute

At Middle Grove School, in the main corridor just inside the front door, a large part of the wall on one side was covered with glass panels. Behind the locked, sliding panels were broad shelves to hold school trophies, pictures, and banners.

Members of basketball, wrestling, track, and baseball teams from the past stared out in dusty silence between displays of ribbons, trophies, and faded banners. Someone long ago had tacked M-I-D-D-L-E G-R-O-V-E in foot-high letters made of construction paper on the wall inside the case.

The principal, Mr. Palmer, loved old photos. Although the newest team photos were displayed in the center, he always made sure old photographs of teams, staff members, and band members were displayed, too. Some of the pictures had been taken more than forty years before.

No one looked at the case much anymore, except to laugh sometimes at the quaint-looking people from the old days.

"Check this out," Adam said to his friend, Jason,

one morning on the way to English class. "Look at these cool dudes." He pointed at a black-and-white photograph of students standing in front of the school door in the 1940s. Many of the boys in the picture had their hair slicked back, flat and shiny, and the girls had skirts on that looked old-fashioned and kind of funny.

"They're probably old now," Jason said. "Years from now they'll say the same thing about us."

"Anyway," Adam said, turning from the case, "let's hurry up and get to Miss Warner's room. I don't want to be late for English."

"You?" Jason turned to his friend and grinned. "*You're* worried about getting to English?"

"There's this incredible new girl," Adam said, lowering his voice and looking around. "Just moved here from Los Angeles. Jimmy Trammel told me. Said he saw her talking to Miss Warner about getting into class. Said she was so fantastic he almost dropped the books he was carrying, right there in the hallway."

Hurrying into 12A—Miss Warner's room—both boys were surprised to find a tall, sandy-haired man sitting behind the desk where Miss Warner usually sat. He was tan and athletic-looking, and about the age of Jason's dad. He offered them a friendly nod as they passed.

"Ah-hah, sub time," Jason said, plopping down in his desk in the second row.

"You got it," said the man, smiling. He glanced at

his watch. "We'll give it a few more minutes," he added, "for people to get here before I take roll."

Jason glanced at Adam in the next desk. He was leaning as far forward as he could to check out the new girl, who had taken a corner desk. Jimmy was right. She was fantastic.

"Anybody see the Cubs and the Pirates play last night?" said the man.

"Yeah," Jason said. "A real nothin' till the sixth inning. Then everything busted loose."

"Sure did," the man said, smiling. "You a Cubs fan?"

"Naw, Angels," Jason said.

"Friend of mine was on the Angels' farm team for a while," the man said. "Pretty good shortstop. Never made it to the majors. Injuries and so-on."

"Yeah, well, Angels haven't done well the last couple of years, but I like 'em anyway," Jason said with a shrug.

"Why not?" The man continued to smile. "Angels have done pretty well during the main season the last couple of years. They've just fallen down a little at the end of the season. I remember a few years ago, they had an 81-62 record going, then wound up the season eight games behind Oakland."

Jason noticed even Adam was no longer trying to see the girl, but instead was listening to what the man was saying.

"Any other sports fans here?" The man looked

around, still smiling. Several students raised their hands. "We'll have to talk about it later," he added. "I love baseball. In fact, I love most sports."

"Miss Warner doesn't know anything about baseball," Adam said.

Jason could tell from Adam's expression that he was delighted to find a teacher so knowledgeable about the game.

"Well, to get to work," the man said, rising. "As most of you already know, I'm your substitute teacher for today. My name is Mr. Blakely. Miss Warner took ill this morning."

"Wouldn't it be great," Adam whispered, "if she never came back and we could get this guy full time?"

Jason nodded and listened as the man continued. "Since Miss Blakely wasn't able to leave me any lesson plans, I've decided we'll go on a little impromptu field trip."

"What the heck does 'impromptu' mean?" Adam whispered.

Mr. Blakely looked at Adam. "For those who don't know that word," he said, " 'impromptu' means sort of on-the-spot or spur-of-the-moment. I just thought it might be instructional and fun to study some of the rock layers and geological formations on the bluffs above the Altar River flats. It's a good place to learn about minerals and rocks, and it's only a few miles or so from here. We'll be back long before school is out."

One of the girls in the class raised her hand. "We always have our parents sign permission slips before field trips," she said. "How can we do that?"

"No need," Mr. Blakely said, smiling again. "I checked with the principal's office, and they granted me general permission for a short trip." He leaned closer and pretended to be speaking secretly. "I'll tell you something," he said. "I grew up around here, and once in a while I used to go up to the Altar bluffs when I played hooky from school. But don't tell anybody I told you that. It's a great place to kill a couple of hours."

"You went to *this* school?" Jason said, forgetting to raise his hand.

"Sure did." Mr. Blakely strolled over to the window and peered out. "Probably find my initials carved around here someplace." After a few moments, he said, "There's a bus waiting at the corner of the parking lot by the side door. Let's head out there, and we'll be on our way. One thing, though. I want you to be absolutely quiet in the hall. No disturbing other classes. If you're *really* quiet, maybe I'll consider stopping for burgers on the way back from the bluffs."

"Fantastic!" Adam whispered as the class moved almost soundlessly toward the side door. "Man, I wish this guy could be here full time! Don't you?"

"No kidding," Jason said. "Miss Warner never does any of this stuff."

When they were all seated in the bus, Mr. Blakely

stepped into the center of the aisle near the front and said, ''I thought we had a driver all ready to go, but I guess not. Looks like we'll have to wait a while.''

After several minutes, he stood up again and said, ''Looks like he's not going to show. If you'll agree to behave and not get rowdy, I can drive the bus. I used to drive one in college. But I can't drive and keep an eye on you, so you'll have to help me on this. Okay?''

''Okay,'' several students said at the same time.

Mr. Blakely was preparing to get into the driver's seat when someone outside began to thump on the bus door. When Mr. Blakely opened the door, a large middle-aged man stepped inside. He had a heavy, dark moustache and wore what looked like a bulky wool shirt and workmen's pants. On his head he had an old-fashioned wool cap. ''I'm your driver,'' the man said to Mr. Blakely. He didn't bother looking around at the students.

Mr. Blakely hesitated for several seconds before speaking. ''Well . . . uh . . . you're not the driver I expected.''

''I'm a substitute driver for today,'' the man said. His tone was flat, and his expression never changed as he spoke.

''Well, I'm a sub myself today,'' Mr. Blakely said. ''I'm a little nervous about switching drivers when we hadn't really planned . . .''

''It's okay,'' the man said. ''I'm licensed, and I have school permission.''

''Well, I guess it's okay then,'' Mr. Blakely said.

He rose slowly and took a seat not far from Adam and Jason.

"Mr. Blakely," Adam said as the bus, with the other man at the wheel, began to pull out of the parking lot, "who do you like better—the Giants or the Athletics?"

"Huh? Oh, I'm sorry," Mr. Blakely said, smiling again at the boys. "I guess my mind was wandering. Oh, I would say Giants. I went crazy when they won the National League pennant a while back. And I even like the Mets. I went crazy when they won the Series in 'eighty-six."

"I like the Athletics," Adam said. "But that's okay." And then to Jason he whispered, "I think Mr. Blakely's worried about that driver dude. Guy *does* look like he could ax-murder about a dozen people and not even lose his appetite."

In less than a quarter of an hour, the bus arrived at a dusty, treeless rest stop near a bend in the Altar River. The entire rest stop consisted of a few scattered picnic tables, a water fountain, and two restrooms. A small footbridge spanned the river in the direction of the high bluffs on the far side.

Mr. Blakely stood up again in the aisle and turned to the students. "Our driver, Mr. . . . uh . . ."

"Jireski," said the man from the driver's seat.

". . . Mr. Jireski," Mr. Blakely continued, "will need to stay with the bus, but the rest of you may follow me across the bridge and up the path you can see over there beyond the river. A little farther down there's a steeper path to the right that comes out on top. There are some caves up there, too, that I can show you. But please, for safety's sake, stay close to me."

"Driver gives me the creeps," Adam said when they had crossed the footbridge. "Glad he's stayin' back."

"He's probably just some guy who minds his own business," Jason said. Then he laughed. "Or maybe he's wanted in twelve states for chopping people up and devouring their flesh."

As they turned up the path toward the top of the bluffs, Jason could still see the driver seated in the bus. What a strange, boring life he must lead, he thought.

Most of the students were puffing by the time the class reached the top. Several of the girls already were complaining about little stones and sand in their shoes. Neither Jason nor Adam had ever seen the river or the bluffs from so high before. It was easily two or three hundred feet from the shelflike surface at the top to the broad, slow-moving river below. The bus was no more than a small, orange rectangle off to one side.

"Well," Mr. Blakely said, puffing a little as he spoke, "was it worth the hike or not?"

"Yeah," several students said.

"Nice view," said one boy.

"Gives me the creeps," one of the girls said. "I hate heights."

"When I was a kid I loved it on the bluff," Mr. Blakely said, sitting down on the flat, rocky surface. "I always felt strong and powerful up here, like I ruled the world or something."

"Did you play a lot of sports when you went to Middle Grove?" Adam said, sitting down beside Mr. Blakely.

Mr. Blakely was still staring out across the river flats. "Yeah. At least I tried out for everything. Baseball, basketball, track. I was skinny and pretty small, though. I had a little trouble because of that."

"Hard to believe you were little and skinny," one of the girls said.

"Well, I was," said Mr. Blakely. "Much too skinny."

"What did they do?" asked Jason, sitting down beside Adam.

Mr. Blakely hesitated, and then shrugged. "I ended up on the wrong end of a lot of practical jokes. Once, some basketball players from school tied me up and took me four or five miles out of town. Then they took all my clothes and ran away. I had to make my way back to town without a stitch on."

"That's terrible!" one of the girls said.

"Pretty rotten joke," Jason said softly. He noticed that Mr. Blakely wasn't smiling now. He seemed to be staring at nothing at all, his gaze drifting above the trees in the valley below.

"Not long after," Mr. Blakely said, his voice little more than a whisper, "there was a fire in the basketball locker room. The coach had left and several players were still inside . . ." His voice trailed off to silence.

"What happened?" Adam asked.

"Some of them . . . died," Mr. Blakely said, still looking off over the valley. "There was smoke, and the door was jammed . . . Coach Davis . . . thought I started it. The police asked a lot of questions. People in town said I was a terrible person . . . and then the police said they couldn't prove anything . . . and then we moved away. Isn't it funny? And all I wanted to do was play on the team like everybody else."

"Why would they pick on you?" one of the girls asked.

"No one else to blame, I guess," Mr. Blakely said, his voice sounding more normal. "That wasn't all, either. One time after the fire, Rick Thomas, who was captain, and some other players locked me in a school closet all night. The janitor found me the next morning. When I got home my dog, Boomer, was gone. I never saw him again."

"That's horrible!" another girl said. "That's just plain horrible!"

"That's okay," Mr. Blakely mumbled. "Lots of their pets disappeared that year. Dogs, cats, even a couple of birds." He smiled a slow, deliberate smile. "They never knew what happened to them."

Adam was beginning to get a strange, uncomfortable feeling in the pit of his stomach. He glanced at Jason, who seemed a little nervous, too.

Now several of the other students, both boys and girls, were gathering around and sitting on the flat surface of the bluff.

"And finally you moved away?" one of the girls asked.

Mr. Blakely's voice was low, and even. "Yeah, finally. And after we moved I started to work out and I got taller. Ended up playing basketball in high school and did pretty well in college. Played three seasons with the Celtics before I wrecked my leg."

"You're kidding!" Jason said. "You really played for Boston?"

Mr. Blakely smiled at Jason. "Sure did," he said. Now he sounded cheerful, like before. "Greatest experience of my life. I'll have to tell you about it sometime." He stood up. "Well, enough of my ancient history. Anybody want to explore a few caves farther up?"

"Sure," several people said, rising to their feet.

"Later, then, can you tell us more about the Celtics?" Jason asked. "I never met anybody before who played pro anything, let alone the *Celtics*. I mean, like, that's as good as you can get."

"Sure, we'll talk about it," Mr. Blakely said, smiling again and turning to the other students. "They say there's some lost money in one of the caves up here. Probably not true, but I've heard rumors about that since I was a kid. Some old-time robbers supposedly hid a lot of money up there. So many caves, it's hard to tell. I used to look for it when I was a kid. So did everybody else. Who knows? Maybe you'll get lucky. If you do, remember you'll have to pay me a reward for telling you about it." He smiled at the group.

"Let's go!" several students said.

"Okay, let's do it," Mr. Blakely said. He took off his suit coat and tossed it onto a nearby rock. It was easy to see he was still in good shape. He moved with the easy, fluid grace of an athlete. Then he turned and led the students away from the bluff, toward a nearby cave.

"Can you believe it?" Jason said to Adam as they followed the other students. "The *Celtics?*"

"Think he's tall enough for pro basketball?" Adam whispered, glancing at the man as he walked.

Jason couldn't get over his excitement. "Are you kidding? There are some guys who aren't even six feet tall in the NBA. Not many, but there are some. What are you talking about?"

"I don't know. He, just, I don't know."

Before they reached the first cave, one of the girls who had run ahead came out of the cave entrance and held up her hand. "Forget it," she said. "Nothing in here. Let's try that one." She pointed at the largest cave entrance nearby.

When Mr. Blakely hesitated, several students, including Adam and Jason, ran ahead and ducked into the opening in the broad, sloping rock face. Inside, they waited until their eyes adjusted to the light. Turning around slowly in the damp, clinging air, they were surprised to discover a large, smooth-walled cave chamber.

As the rest of the students rushed to join them, their voices, one by one, faded almost to silence. Before the students, framed by a pair of cold, mostly burned-down candles on silver candlesticks, was a broad, rough-sawn table on which were piled dozens of bleached-white small-animal bones. Resting on the bones, like some strange, primitive sacrifice, was a brand-new leather basketball.

Behind the students, at the cave entrance, Mr. Blakely's voice rose, echoing on the cave walls. It was thin and reedy, not full and smooth like before, and its eerie sound made the hair stand up on Adam's neck.

"Coach Davis?" the voice said. "Coach Davis, they were mean to me. Don't you remember? Rick Thomas and the others? Please. Don't you understand? They were mean to me."

"My gosh!" Jason whispered. "Is he kidding?"

"I don't think so." Adam tried to peek at Mr. Blakely's face without being obvious about it. Mr. Blakely had a curious, childlike expression. He was staring past the students at a blank area in the rear of the cave.

"We gotta get the heck out of here," Jason said, forgetting to lower his voice. At the sound of Jason's voice, Mr. Blakely turned and stared in the direction of Adam and Jason.

"Rick?" Mr. Blakely said to Jason. "Why, Rick? Why were you so mean?" His expression was still strange and blank.

"What . . . are the bones for?" Adam asked, his voice shaking. "Is this your cave?"

"Lots of dogs and cats," Mr. Blakely said, almost whispering again, his expression still blank. "Lots of people's dogs and cats."

Several of the girls were on the verge of tears. "Please, can we go down to the bus now?" one of the girls said. "Please, Mr. Blakely?"

"There is only one path down from here," Mr. Blakely finally said, "and I'm between you and that path. No one can go down. We have to wait until Coach Davis says we can go." His eyes were narrowing to steely points of light, and his jaw was tight. The bulky muscles in his arms rippled as he backed slowly out of the cave and headed down the slope. He was still between the students and the path down to the bus.

"Mr. Blakely, why are you . . ." Adam began.

"Quiet!" Mr. Blakely shouted, fixing him with a hard, cold-metal stare. "Nobody goes until we get permission."

Students nervously followed Mr. Blakely until they

had reached the flat, smooth rock on which they had sat before.

Motioning for them all to sit down, Mr. Blakely paced in a small circle for a few moments, then stopped abruptly. "Who knows Bill Dorman?" he said.

"Uhh, that's my dad's name," Jason said.

Mr. Blakely again was silent for a moment. "Forrest Taggart?"

"Uh . . . my dad," one boy said softly.

"Tom Petrocelli?"

"My . . . dad."

Most of the students' eyes were now wide with a mixture of surprise, curiosity, and fear.

"Mr. Blakely, can we please go?" Jason said, trying to sound as calm as he could.

Mr. Blakely whirled around and stepped closer to where Jason was seated on the rock surface with the others. "You keep quiet!" he shouted. "You keep your mouth *shut!*"

Almost instantly Mr. Blakely turned away from Jason again and began to stare, as before, out across the broad, sloping valley below them. This time, when he spoke, his voice was little more than a whisper. "Boomer was my best friend in the whole world," he said. "There wasn't anything he wouldn't do for me. When he didn't come home, I looked in every street, alley, and backyard in town . . . There wasn't even anything I could bury."

"It's too bad your dog got killed and they were mean to you and stuff, but we didn't have anything to do with that," said Julie, who was seated near Jason. She was small and thin for her age.

Mr. Blakely stepped closer. "You aren't even on the team, are you?" he said softly.

She moved her head slowly from side to side, her face flushed with fear.

Mr. Blakely suddenly reached down, grabbed her by the arm, yanked her to her feet, then took both arms and lifted her high above his head as she and several other girls screamed.

"The rest of you, don't even think about trying to run away," Mr. Blakely shouted. "You do, and I'll pitch her over the edge. And I'm still between you and the path."

All of the students were frozen in terror.

"It's important to be on the team," Mr. Blakely said. "I think people who aren't on the team shouldn't even be here. I could be on the team. They *want* me to play."

"*Please!*" Julie screamed. "Please put me *down!*"

Mr. Blakely seemed to teeter near the edge for a few seconds. Finally, he lowered Julie, still crying, to the rock surface. He was becoming more agitated now, pacing faster, and the students could see perspiration forming on his neck and arms.

"Basketball is important," he said, half-shouting. "Every kid should have a chance to play."

As Mr. Blakely spoke, Jason became aware of a shadow and then a form, moving out from between the two boulders shielding the path leading up from the river.

Mr. Blakely walked to the edge of the rock table overlooking the river, and stared as before at the broad, silent valley. When he did so, the shadow near the boulders moved again, and the students saw that it was Mr. Jireski, the substitute bus driver. Mr. Jireski was a big, powerful-looking man who still seemed as crabby and mean as he had when he'd brought the students here an hour or so before. As he stepped silently into the open, Mr. Jireski put a finger to his lips, motioning for the students to remain quiet and not say anything about his presence.

"Even my own father . . ." Mr. Blakely said, still staring into the valley. "Even he was ashamed of me. After the fire, people whispered and talked about me behind my back. They were glad my dog was gone . . . I wanted them *all* to be dead . . ."

Mr. Jireski moved in silence toward the spot near the edge of the bluff where Mr. Blakely still stood. Most of the students by now were almost afraid to breathe, for fear the sound would cause Mr. Blakely to turn around. All sat rigid and unmoving, trying to see Mr. Jireski without moving their heads.

"I'm going to get even with all of you . . ." Mr. Blakely said, whirling around. As he did so, he caught a blur of motion as Mr. Jireski tackled him. They both fell to the rocky surface of the bluff, no more than a foot or two from the edge and the sheer drop to the boulders and river. As they struggled furiously, the students scrambled back, away from the edge. Many began to sprint toward the path leading down to the river.

As the men continued to struggle, the rest of the students jumped up and ran.

Jason and Adam, as they neared the path, stopped and turned back to look just as both men got to their feet and began pounding each other with their fists. They heard the swack! of Mr. Blakely's fist as it slammed the side of Mr. Jireski's head. Mr. Blakely swung again and missed, and as he did so, Mr. Jireski landed a powerful punch directly in the middle of Mr. Blakely's face. The force of the blow knocked him off his feet and as he flew backward, he tumbled straight off the edge of the sheer rock cliff. Mr. Blakely's body seemed to drift in the sudden silence for two or three seconds before slamming hard against the rocky surface of the river flats far below. Several girls who already had reached the flats screamed in terror.

"This is horrible!" Adam moaned to Jason. "I don't believe it! The driver killed him!"

Mr. Jireski stood still for several seconds, staring at the edge of the cliff. He finally turned to the boys and motioned for them to go on down the path. Adam and Jason turned and began to run, stopping only when they reached the door of the bus, still parked in the same spot in the rest area. Both were puffing so hard they couldn't speak for a minute or two. The door was open, and the other students already were seated on board. Many of them were still crying, and all looked frightened.

Within minutes, Mr. Jireski stepped onto the bus, glanced at the students without speaking, then slipped into the driver's seat, started the engine and headed the bus out of the rest area toward the highway.

"What will they do about Mr. Blakely?" several students said anxiously.

"I bet he never played for the Celtics at all," said another. Adam and Jason signaled them to be quiet. For the rest of the trip into town, no one spoke.

As the bus pulled into the main school parking lot, the students could see four police cars parked near the principal's office. Mr. Jireski swung the bus around, near the police cars, and brought it to a stop at the curb. When he opened the door, the students jumped from their seats and bolted for the door, jostling each other in the process. They streamed into the hallway, past the glass trophy cases, where several police officers were talking to Mr. Palmer, the principal, and Mrs. Garretz, the assistant principal.

"Wait, wait, wait!" Mr. Palmer shouted to the students. "Please stay right here for a moment." It was easy to tell he was both shocked and relieved to see the class. "Is everyone here?" he asked, scanning the group. His voice sounded nervous and strained.

"Yes, except for the driver, Mr. Jireski," Jason said.

"Is he the one who took you?" asked one of the police officers, as two officers turned and ran toward the door to the parking lot.

"No, no," several students said, their words tumbling together. "The substitute teacher, Mr. Blakely, wanted to take us out to the rock bluffs above the Altar River flats for an outing. Mr. Jireski just got on the bus and said he was a substitute driver. He's the one who brought us back here. Mr. Blakely got all crazy at the river, and Mr. Jireski fought with him, and . . ."

"Hold on. Wait a minute," one of the officers said. "First of all, who is Mr. Blakely?"

"The sub," several students said.

"Yeah," Adam said. "Miss Warner got sick, I guess, just before school, and Mr. Blakely came to fill in. Then he got the idea to go on an outing, 'cause Miss Warner hadn't left him any lesson plans, so . . ."

"So that's the story he gave the kids," the officer said, turning to Mr. Palmer. "He must have tied up Miss Warner in her apartment before coming over to the school."

"*Tied her up?*" Jason and Adam said at the same time.

"Mr. Blakely was NOT an assigned substitute

teacher," Mr. Palmer said. "He came into your room without the principal's office even knowing about it, and he even managed to get you all onto a bus. I don't know how it happened, but we're still checking on it."

The officer turned and began to speak more softly to Mr. Palmer, but Adam could still hear him. "We think Blakely is the same maniac who killed a retired basketball coach and his wife on vacation near San Francisco last year. Police fished them and their car out of the bay. I'd say these kids here are *real* lucky."

"By the way," said Mr. Palmer, "where *is* Mr. Blakely?"

"That's what we were trying to tell you," Adam said. "Mr. Blakely's back on the river flats. Dead. Mr. Jireski fought with him because Mr. Blakely was getting crazy and threatening to throw some of us off the bluff. He said he had trouble when he was a kid and some basketball team members got killed and they thought he did it and later he was a pro basketball player and a bunch of other stuff. I don't believe he ever played basketball at all. He and Mr. Jireski fought and he hit Mr. Jireski and Mr. Jireski hit him back and Mr. Blakely went over the edge."

"This is a nightmare," Mr. Palmer said. "And you say Mr. Blakely fell to the river flats?"

"Sounds like our psycho," one of the officers said.

"I don't understand it," Jason said. "At first he sounded like a really nice guy. Knew all about sports.

Said maybe we'd all get burgers on the way home."

"I'll send a unit out there right away," one officer said, heading for the door. "Where's this Jireski?"

"Out in the bus yet, I guess," Adam said. "We all kind of ran out of the bus pretty fast."

Before the officer reached the door, the one who had left earlier stepped back into the hallway. "No one out there," he said. "Just the empty bus."

"Wait a minute," another officer said, running for the door. "He's got to be out there. He can't have gone far."

"You boys and girls stay right here," Mr. Palmer said, "until the police have searched around the school. Why don't you just sit down along the wall right here, and we'll have you on your way home in a few minutes." He still sounded nervous, and he was sweating.

As the students were sliding to the floor against the wall, two men entered the hallway from the front parking lot. One carried several cameras.

"*Times-Dispatch*," one of the men said to Mr. Palmer. "Are you the principal?"

Mr. Palmer nodded and ushered the men into his office, away from the students.

"Unbelievable," Adam said, unwrapping a stick of gum.

"I wonder how long we'll have to sit here," one girl said. "I just want to go home."

"And I thought the guy was so nice, knowin' so

much about sports and all," Adam said. He glanced at Jason, who was leaning back against the wall with his eyes closed.

"Yeah. Me, too," Jason mumbled.

"Maybe Mr. Jireski is hiding someplace," Adam said. "He's some tough fighter."

Through the office windows they could see Mr. Palmer talking with the two men from the newspaper. Several policemen came into the hallway and began opening doors to several rooms and peering inside. "You kids didn't see Mr. Jireski come through here, did you?" one of the officers asked.

"No," several students said.

"Can we go pretty soon?" Adam asked when an officer came out of one of the rooms.

"Won't be long." The policemen headed down the hallway, opening more doors.

"This is boring," Adam mumbled. He stood up, thrust his hands in his pockets, turned around and began idly looking at the photos in the trophy case above the heads of the seated students.

A minute or so later, Jason heard Adam gasp and go tense as he suddenly pressed his face closer to the glass panel of the trophy case. "Jason!" Adam said in a hoarse half-whisper. "Jason! Get up here! Look at this!"

"Hey, I'm tired," Jason grumbled without opening his eyes.

"Jason!" Adam said again, and gave his friend a

gentle boot with his foot. "I'm not kidding! Stand up and look at this!"

Slowly, reluctantly, Jason rose to his feet and turned around. Several other students, now curious, also stood and strained to see what Adam was talking about.

Following the direction of Adam's pointing finger, Jason focused on a slightly curled black-and-white photograph tacked to the wall of the case among several dusty trophies. The photo showed band members standing with a driver beside a Middle Grove School bus. A sign held by two of the band members said "Middle Grove School Band, 1954."

The driver, standing near the bus door, was Mr. Jireski. There was no mistaking the figure. He had the same heavy, dark moustache in the picture, and was wearing the same bulky wool shirt, workmen's pants, and old-fashioned wool cap he'd worn when he had driven the students to the river bluff.

"Wait a minute . . ." Jason said. "That's almost forty years . . ."

"Oh, my gosh!" Adam said, his voice wavering. "Look!" He was pointing at an engraved metal plate mounted on a walnut plaque just below the photo. The engraving on the plate said, "In loving memory of the friend and bus driver who always took care of us—Walter Jireski, 1897–1959. From the students and staff of Middle Grove School . . ."

The Mailbox

As far as people in this city go, I'm probably as much of a native as you can get.

I mean, I was *born* in Bangor (which is in Maine, in case you've never been in this part of the country) and here I am starting my teenage years and I haven't really gone anywhere yet. Well, yeah, my folks and I went down to Bar Harbor and took the ferry to Yarmouth once. That's in Nova Scotia, which is in Canada. It took a long time and my best friend, Gina, and I got seasick and threw up and stuff, but it's still not as though I've really *gone* somewhere, like, say, to New York or Kansas City. Not that I have any *reason* to go to Kansas City, but you know what I mean.

When I said this once to a couple of people who weren't from here, they chirped, "Well, young lady, why would you want to go anywhere when you're surrounded by *so much* right here?"

That part's true, I suppose. We're on the Penobscot

River, which is pretty big, and the Kenduskeag Stream runs right through town. We've got tons of places to ski (I'm sort of okay at downhilling), and in the summer there's a jillion places to go. There are so many lakes and streams and forests and deer and partridge and long, white beaches and stony cliffs and capes and hidden coves and everything else, I'm sure nobody ever even counted it all. Or if they did, it must have taken them absolutely forever.

And it's all pretty nice. I mean, I would think you'd have to go really far to find anything like Bar Harbor as a really pretty place to be. It's why they get so many people in the summer. We get a lot of people visiting in Bangor, too, because this part of the country's so nice. Most people are okay, whether they're just visiting or actually moving here from someplace else.

But a few *aren't* okay. Like the man who bought the McCordale House last year. Around here, when an old house is very special or large or it belonged to somebody who was very important, everyone calls it by the original owner's name.

The McCordale House is kind of close to where I live. It was built by this guy named Dr. McCordale almost a hundred years ago. Supposedly he came from a pretty rich family in Boston. In Bangor he ended up owning a lumber company, a hardware store, and part of a shipping company. And every day he still went to his clinic and treated patients because he just liked being a doctor, I guess. He sure didn't need the money.

Although it's always been called the McCordale House, it's had tons of owners since McCordale, and some of them allowed it to sort of fall apart. I always thought that was a shame. McCordale built it with lots of shutters and two big brick fireplaces and columns across a porch in the front and a white railing above the porch. He put in all hardwood floors and real expensive paneling and stuff, too.

Some people have said the place was haunted. When I was younger, I never thought much of those stories. Heck, somebody's *always* talking about this or that house being haunted. If half the houses people claim are haunted really were, there'd be more haunted houses than there are ghosts.

The man and his wife who bought it last summer were from New York. Even before they moved in, I heard from one of my best friends (who heard it from her mother) that they were planning to tear it down.

My mom says I'm far too nosy for my own good. Just the same, I was curious to know what they were going to build in place of the old house, so I decided I'd see if I could meet the new owners. My mom said I should leave them alone. I was still curious, so I walked past several times until one day I saw them outside.

"I'm Coby Anderson from right over there," I said,

pointing in the direction of our house. "I'm your neighbor, sort of."

Both the man and the woman nodded. "Hi," the man mumbled. Then they both turned away and went on with their work. The man had a sketch pad, and it looked like maybe they were drawing a few different design ideas—ideas, I suppose, for new houses that might fit in with the trees and shrubs on the lot.

I decided to be direct. "Are you going to tear this house down?" I asked. "I heard you were, and I just wondered."

"Could be," the man said without turning around.

"I read all about Dr. McCordale who built it," I offered. "He was mayor for a while a long, long time ago and he even ran for the United States Senate. I guess they used to have lots of parties, and even some famous people came here, and . . ."

"Look, we have some things to do," the man interrupted, turning to me. "Maybe we can talk another time."

Later, I called my friend, Gina, to tell her about the house.

"What were the new owners like?" she asked.

"Kinda rude," I said. "At least the guy."

"Well, maybe they didn't mean to be," she said. "Maybe they just had a lot on their minds."

I decided maybe that was the case, so a couple of weeks later, I walked past the McCordale place again.

The lady was measuring something or other on the house.

"Hello again," I said, trying to sound as nice as possible.

"Hello," she said, and smiled. She sure seemed nicer than her husband.

"My dad says maybe these oak trees are the same ones Dr. McCordale planted," I said.

"I wouldn't know," the lady said. "They certainly are beautiful, aren't they?"

I was hoping I could keep the conversation going, and maybe get around to whether they were really going to tear the house down, and why. "I know quite a bit about this house," I said. "It's been here all my life, of course."

"And much longer," she said, smiling again.

"I remember when they put up your mailbox," I said, looking about for anything to talk about. "That was only a couple of years ago. The Taylors owned this house then. Mr. Taylor was old and kind of grumpy. He didn't want anyone hitting the post the box sits on and knocking it over, so he put the box on that big, hollow steel post that it's on and he sank it into the ground and he filled the post with cement. The box itself is pretty much of an antique, they said."

"My, you certainly know a lot about this place," the lady said, walking to the edge of the sidewalk and examining the box and the post on which it rested.

"Most houses around here have mailboxes attached to them," I offered. "I guess you have a post and box because your house sits back farther."

"You're very observant," the lady said, turning first to her shrubs, then back to me again. "By the way, I'm Mrs. Aurmont. We'll have to visit again, Coby."

"Why didn't you ask her about tearing down the place?" Gina asked later when we talked on the phone.

"I don't know. She seemed so nice, I didn't want to seem *too* pushy . . ."

Several days later I was riding my bike when I saw Mr. and Mrs. Aurmont out in the yard again. After talking with Mrs. Aurmont, I felt as though we were almost friends.

"I can help you with some of the measuring and stuff if you like," I said, leaning my bike against one of the big oak trees.

"No, that won't be necessary," Mr. Aurmont said without smiling. He was an intense-looking little man with a bald head and a bushy black moustache. "Please tell your friends I don't want anyone poking around this place when we're away, either. We'll have heavy equipment coming in soon to start tearing the house down and we don't want someone hurt."

Then it's true, I thought. They *are* tearing it down.

"Thank you for offering your help," Mrs. Aurmont said, smiling as I left.

Boy, I thought, what a grouch. How does she stand to live with someone like him?

"My dad said he heard they're going to put in a bigger, brand-new house, and it'll even have a tennis court in the back," Gina said later. "My dad heard it from a contractor he knows."

For the next couple of weeks, I didn't talk to Mr. or Mrs. Aurmont. Some days, I noticed Mrs. Aurmont in the yard, but most of the time it appeared no one was at the house at all.

One day I was riding my bike again, and I stopped in front of the place, wishing I might find Mrs. Aurmont outside again. At least *she* was a nice person. I leaned my bike against the mailbox support post and just stood there a while, wondering what the new house would look like. Probably big and fancy, with lots of wide windows and maybe one of those classy carved doors in front. And I couldn't forget the tennis court. Wow, what a place it was going to be. Probably was going to make the neighbors mad, though, because they had all these old, historic houses. A new one among those would stand out quite a bit.

Turning to leave, I glanced at the old mailbox again. It certainly was an antique, with a faded metal flag on the side and a fancy little curlicue for a handle. You could tell the box had been painted about a million times before. I absentmindedly pulled on the little handle and flipped open the box. Inside was what looked like a rolled-up piece of paper with a lot of handwriting on it, in ink.

I admit I was curious. I mean, it wasn't like it was a letter or something, and I wasn't, like, opening somebody else's mail. It was just a piece of paper, right there for anybody to see. When I took it out of the box, I realized there were several sheets of paper inside, all filled with curious, old-fashioned, fancy handwriting. And the ink looked like the old-fashioned liquid kind, not ballpoint or felt-tip.

Whoever had written them had a real flowery way of describing things, too. On the pages were all sorts of descriptions of parts of the house, how this or that kind of oak was used in this room or that room, and how pine was used somewhere else and how some of the paneling was black walnut here, and Philippine mahogany there. There were facts and figures about the cost of bricks and marble and other materials. The last page was like a little diary, with dates when the house was started, when it was completed, and so forth. It was all in the 1880s and '90s.

"This house was built with respect, and dignity, and care," the last page said. "It must be treated the same way—not destroyed." I got a chill. These sounded like they came from old Dr. McCordale—but he'd been *dead* for a long time.

I couldn't wait to show the pages to Mr. and Mrs. Aurmont. I figured they'd flip out when they saw all this stuff. It was really weird the way it was just lying there, in the box, with no envelope or stamp or anything.

I carried the pages up to the front door and knocked, in case they were home, although they hadn't been around very much lately. I was surprised when Mr. Aurmont came to the door.

"Uhh . . . these . . . I noticed these in your old mailbox out there and I thought you might want to have them," I stammered. Then I added, "I didn't try to go looking in your mail or anything."

"In our mailbox?" Mr. Aurmont said, looking very much like he doubted that I was telling the truth. He took the papers from me and quickly shuffled through them, nodding a little and scowling as he scanned the words.

"Well," he said finally, turning to me and wadding up the papers as he spoke, "I'd like to make something clear."

I nodded.

"These obviously weren't mailed, since there's no envelope and no stamp. I don't believe you got them from the mailbox. My guess is you found them here, either in the house or in the garage. You have no right poking about our property. I told you before about leaving things strictly alone." The more he spoke, the angrier he seemed to become.

"No, really," I protested. "They *were* in the mailbox. I didn't snoop around."

"Just the same," said Mr. Aurmont, "you have

been warned." He turned and closed the door in my face.

Same mean old grouch, I thought, as I rode away on my bike.

Just as before, I didn't see either of them for a while after that. I figured there was no use getting Mr. Aurmont any angrier than he already was.

I had to ride past the house to get to my house, though. One day as I came near, I noticed a small, dark cat sitting near the street, staring intently at the Aurmonts' mailbox. The door of the box hung open. Suddenly, the little cat crouched down and then leaped upward and into the open end of the box just as slick as you please. He just disappeared in a flash, tail and all.

"Some trick," I said aloud, smiling and pulling my bike to a stop at the edge of the street. "Let's get you out of that box, kitty, before somebody closes the door and you're trapped." I walked over, reached gently inside—and found nothing at all.

"Wait a minute," I said, swinging my hand around inside and even hitting it on the far end of the box. I looked inside and out and even stepped aside to scan a nearby tree, in case my eyes had played tricks on me and he was up there.

No cat, anywhere. Now I *was* beginning to feel weird. Clearly, something pretty strange was going on here. This time I wasn't going to tell the Aurmonts.

I knew they wouldn't believe it. In fact, I scarcely believed it myself.

I began checking the box every couple of days or so, when I thought they wouldn't notice. I even got pretty good at riding past, nice and slow, and flipping the door open without getting off my bike. Every time I did, I found another piece of paper with the same handwriting on it. I saved the pages and hid them under my bed at home. I didn't even show my parents. I knew they'd think I made it all up.

Whoever was writing the stuff sure knew a lot about the original owner, old Dr. McCordale. There was stuff about how he and his wife enjoyed sailing and "musical evenings" with their two "fair and winsome" daughters, as the writer put it, until "the eldest, despondent over the loss of her beau in a lumbering accident, cast herself from a cruel and lonely seaside cliff and was swallowed in Neptune's mighty roar, never to be seen, nor heard, again."

Another time the writer told of an accident in which a cat darted from the side of the road and frightened the horse pulling Dr. McCordale's buggy, causing the buggy to overturn and breaking the doctor's leg.

The more pages I collected, the more I worried about what to do with them. I couldn't just keep them. Sooner or later, my mom would find them, or someone would see me opening the box or something. I decided I had to show them to Mr. and Mrs. Aurmont. If I showed them to my parents, they'd probably ground me until I was about eighty-two years old.

Instead of taking all of the notes to show them, I took only a couple. As soon as I showed them to Mr. Aurmont, I knew it was a mistake.

"Where *really* did you get these?" he asked, scowling at me and leaning closer.

"In the mailbox. I really did. Somebody just puts them in there."

"Whether you found these in the mailbox or—more likely—while sneaking about this house when we're away, I've had enough of this," he said, his voice rising. "I'm calling your parents, and then I may call the police."

I could feel the tears coming to my eyes. "Please, Mr. Aurmont," I said, my voice wavering, "I haven't gone into your house, and I didn't steal any mail. I just looked at a few of these pages. Please don't call the police. Please." He seemed determined to call *somebody*, so I figured it was better if it were my parents.

My dad and mom came over and apologized to the Aurmonts and said they'd make certain I never bothered them again. I could tell by the tone of my dad's voice that he was pretty mad at me. He yelled a lot when we got home, and I ended up losing my phone privileges for a month.

I knew it was downright dangerous, but I still had the worst urge to peek inside the mailbox. For about a week I resisted the urge; finally I couldn't stand it anymore.

One afternoon on my way home, I swung close to the box and peeked inside. Sure enough, there was another piece of paper. "Tell the woman of the house," it said, "that she should see a doctor about her back problem. It may well be more serious than she thinks."

I thought about this one for several days. If I told anyone, I'd get in *real* trouble. If I didn't, maybe something terrible would happen to nice Mrs. Aurmont's back. The next time I saw her in the yard alone I decided to take a chance.

"Would you mind if I tell you a secret?" I asked, making certain Mr. Aurmont was not around.

"Why, not at all, dear," she said, smiling.

"I guess I'd like you to promise you won't tell Mr. Aurmont or my folks."

"I don't know if I can do that." She stared at me for a moment, and smiled again. "Well, okay. I won't tell."

"You should see a doctor about your back problem," I said. "It could be a lot more serious than you thought."

For a moment, she didn't say a word. "My goodness!" she said finally. "How did you know about *that?* I haven't told anyone about my back, other than my husband."

"Well, please don't tell," I said. "It sounds kinda

weird. But I looked in the mailbox again, and there was a paper in there that said I should tell you that. Oh, yeah. It said something else, too. It said it would be very, very wrong to tear down this house."

Mrs. Aurmont stared at me for several seconds. "Well," she said, "I don't know anything about that mailbox. I do know something strange is going on here."

"Anyway, please don't tell anybody I told you," I said.

"I promised, so I won't," she said. She still had a strange expression on her face.

After that, I began to find other notes. A lot of it was about all the people who had lived in the house over the years. Whoever was writing the notes seemed to be pretty observant—and interested in details about peoples' lives.

One day I found a note that absolutely turned my blood as cold as the north Atlantic in January. "Please be aware," it said, "that the master of the house has taken out several substantial insurance policies on his poor, unfortunate wife, whom he plans to kill, after which it is his intent to burn the house to the ground. He is a thoroughly unscrupulous and avaricious scoundrel."

I didn't know what a few of those words meant, but sure as heck knew what the note meant. Mrs. Aurmont was in a whole pile of danger. I was all the more worried because I hadn't seen her in a while.

I sure was relieved one day when I noticed her alone outside, just as before. When I rode up, she smiled real big and came over to me.

"I saw one of the best doctors in New England about my back, and he agreed that it was very fortunate that I came in when I did," she said. "I have you to thank, although I still don't understand."

I hated to spoil her good mood, but I just couldn't keep quiet about her husband's plans. I asked her to promise again not to say anything about me and the notes. When I told her about the most recent note, you could see she half-believed me and half-didn't believe me. She didn't say much at all, and seemed to be kind of sorting everything out in her mind. I felt pretty awful telling about the murder plans. I really did.

"The stuff about the back problem was true and that came from the mailbox, too," I said. "I guess I'm just saying you maybe should be kinda careful."

She just turned and walked into the house. Her friendly smile had faded and I felt like about the lowest thing on earth. On the other hand, I couldn't have stood not to tell her.

Well, I sure wasn't prepared for the rest of what happened, I have to tell you.

In spite of her promise to me, Mrs. Aurmont finally decided to talk to her husband about the plot idea (she told me this later). I'm sure she was hoping it would all turn out to be just a hoax or a joke and it would all come clear and they could have a big laugh about it. I mean, nobody really wants to believe somebody you love is trying to do you in.

Mr. Aurmont really hit the roof, especially when Mrs. Aurmont finally admitted that the idea of a plot came from me and the mailbox. She said he stormed around and swore and threatened to call the police, just like before. Said he was gonna call my dad and put up a fence and buy a vicious dog and wring my neck and that was just the *start* of what he was going to do to me.

But first he said he was gonna rip out that mailbox once and for all—just tear it out of the ground and trash the thing. Said he'd planned to do just that all along, because he didn't want some beat-up old antique mailbox in front of his new house after it was built, anyway.

He sweated and strained and just about threw himself out of gear entirely, just trying to get that heavy, cement-filled post out of the ground. He was more than a little stubborn. He swore he'd do it himself with no help, thank you very much, even if it killed him.

By a strange twist of fate, that's exactly what it did.

He wrestled that big, heavy post out of the ground and managed to get it standing on end, much taller than he was, on the front sidewalk. As he was standing there, balancing the thing and trying to plan his next move, Mrs. Aurmont came out the front door.

Unfortunately, Mr. Aurmont hadn't lost a bit of the anger that had driven him to yank the post from the ground in the first place. Hearing her come out, he turned to snarl something at her. About then, I came riding by on my bike, not knowing exactly what was going on at the moment. He turned from her, spotted me, and his face lit up like a red light.

"You nosy little brat," he yelled, "you've got no more reason to come around here—ever." As he said that, he forgot that he was hanging onto the post, and he took a couple of steps toward me, poking his finger in my direction as he walked.

He never made the third step. That cement-filled steel post, with the antique mailbox still attached way up on top, teetered on its end for a moment and then came crashing over, crunching his bald little head like a ripe melon.

It was awful. Mrs. Aurmont yelled and I yelled and I ran back to our house to call for help and a lot of neighbors came out to help Mr. Aurmont and it was a real mess. But there was nothing that could help him.

Well, Mrs. Aurmont felt terrible about Mr. Aurmont's death. She started making plans right away to move back to New York. She got another terrible surprise a week or two later, though, when she was going through papers and things in her husband's office. Turns out he *did* have big, fat life insurance policies on her, which meant that if *she*'d died, he would have collected like crazy.

"I knew he had some kind of insurance on me," she told me later, "but I guess I never realized it was so much. Makes a person think a little about the note in the mailbox."

After things settled down a bit, I offered to help Mrs. Aurmont with some of her chores, and we got to be pretty good friends. She was not interested in building a fancy new house the way Mr. Aurmont had been, so I helped her fix up the old one to help get it ready for sale. My dad and I helped her get that post and antique mailbox back into its old spot, and I gave it a brand-new coat of black paint.

When there was no longer any chance of the old house being torn down, it seemed to take on a different atmosphere. The place simply didn't feel the same as before. Mrs. Aurmont said she felt the change, too. It just felt better, somehow. In fact, she scrapped her plans to move back to New York, and decided she might just live here for a while.

Something else was kind of interesting: Although I admit that for a while I peeked into the old mailbox from time to time, looking for more notes written in that familiar, old-fashioned handwriting, I never found another one. To this day, I still haven't found any more.

And you want to know something? That suits me just fine.